A HIGHLAND CHRISTMAS

A CHRISTIAN ROMANCE BOOK 5 IN THE SHADOWS SERIES

JULIETTE DUNCAN

COPYRIGHT

CHAPTER 1

*G*lasgow, Scotland 23 December, 1988

AFTER ALMOST THREE years of working full-time with rape victims, Brianna deserved a holiday. But instead of going with her friend, Susan, to the south of Spain, where the weather would be mild and possibly even warm, she was going to the Scottish Highlands to spend Christmas with her Irish family she barely knew. *Argh!* No, that wasn't quite true—she did know and love some of them, *but the others?* She barely remembered her younger siblings, Aislin, Alana, Brendan and Shawn, after being separated from them when she was just ten following their Mam's untimely death.

Drat Danny for organising this. The one year she'd planned a real holiday. Brianna blew out a breath as a familiar car horn sounded from the road. Drawing back the thin, sheer curtain, she glanced out the window of the two-bedroom semi-detached terraced home in downtown Glasgow she shared with Susan. Although less than eager, she was packed and ready to go, so she flicked the television off, slipped her coat on and stepped outside, closing the door behind her. As the damp air hit her face, Brianna shivered and dreamed of warmer climates.

Lifting her hand, Brianna waved at her brother-in-law, Ryan, as he climbed out of his large SUV and jogged up the stairs towards her. Ryan gave her a quick kiss before grabbing her bag and placing it in the boot. Brianna slid into the back seat behind her older sister, Grace, rubbing her hands together.

Grace turned around and extended her slender hand, giving Brianna's a squeeze. "Hey, Bibi, how are you doing?"

Brianna shivered, her lips tight. "Wishing I was in Spain." She sounded petty, and she had to get over it, but at least she could be honest with Grace.

"Don't we all?" Grace laughed lightly as she patted Brianna's hand. "Never mind, it'll be good to see everyone after all this time."

Brianna humphed as she strapped herself in. "I don't know about that. I'd been looking forward to having a real holiday for once."

"Next year, maybe." Grace gave Brianna an understanding smile before facing the front and cranking the heat up, while Ryan jumped in and pulled away from the kerb.

Brianna stared out the window as dreary terraced houses flashed past. She was being immature. Grace was probably right... spending Christmas together for the first time in more than twenty years should be cause for celebration. Brianna just didn't feel it. She didn't want to rake over the past—goodness knows she'd done enough of that and now she'd moved on. In fact, she'd even been thinking of leaving the Rape Centre she and Grace ran together, although the courage to share that thought with Grace was lacking.

With no other option, Brianna settled into the soft leather seat for the two and a half-hour drive to Fort William and the Christian community her older brother, Danny, and his wife, Lizzy, managed, and dreamed she was in a plane heading for Spain, not a car heading for the Highlands in thick, damp fog.

∼

"YOU NEED TO LEAVE NOW, Daniel, or you'll be late." Lizzy folded her arms and studied her husband with amusement as he stood in front of the mirror combing his dark, wavy hair.

"I know, love, I'm almost ready." Daniel caught her eye in the hallway mirror and winked as he slipped the comb into the back pocket of his faded blue jeans and turned to face her. "Sure you can't come?"

As he lifted an eyebrow while rubbing her forearms and gazing into her eyes, Lizzy almost changed her mind. But no... she had to stay home and finish the preparations. "You know I can't come. Mother and Father will be here soon. Besides, the children are looking forward to going to the airport with you."

Daniel stepped closer and drew her into an embrace, nuzzling her neck. "Okay, but I'll miss you."

Lizzy chuckled and shook her head. "Don't be silly—you'll

only be gone a few hours." She pulled back and looked into his crystal blue eyes, her voice growing serious. "Just take care on those roads, especially in this fog."

"I fully intend to." Daniel lowered his face and placed a soft kiss on her lips. "Sorry I won't be here to help with everything."

"No, you're not! Since when did you like cooking?"

Daniel laughed. "You're right."

"Thank you. Now, off with you!" Lizzy pushed him away and stepped into the living room where the children were running around chasing each other. The noise was deafening. "Dillon, James, Clare, calm down. Daddy's ready. Come and give me a hug."

They all ran towards Lizzy at once, wrapping their arms around her, almost toppling her over. Lizzy laughed and met Daniel's amused gaze. "I think I'm glad I'm staying here. It's going to be a noisy trip!"

"It's all good, love. I can make as much noise as they can."

"I know. That's what I mean." Lizzy let out another laugh, but a tinge of sadness flowed through her. It would have been fun to take a drive with Daniel and the children, but there was a ton of cooking to do, and besides, her parents were coming, and no doubt they'd be early. She bent down and pulled the children into a group hug. "Have a nice time together, darlings, and I'll have some surprises waiting for you when you get home."

Five-year-old Clare pulled on Lizzy's arm. "Surprises, Mummy? Like what?"

"It wouldn't be a surprise if I told you. Now, give me another hug and off you go."

Lizzy helped the children into their coats and into the bus belonging to the Elim Community, the Christian community she and Daniel had managed for the past five years. She waved as Daniel headed the bus towards the main building to collect his older brother, Caleb, who lived in the community with his wife, Caitlin, and their two daughters. Caleb was going with Daniel and the children to the airport in Inverness to meet the four siblings arriving from Ireland. She stopped waving within seconds as the tail-lights disappeared into the thick pea-soup fog they'd woken up to. As she stared into the thick mist, Lizzy shivered and prayed for their safety. Not even the grand manor house was visible... she'd never seen it so thick.

With Daniel and the children gone, Lizzy quickly tidied up before scurrying down the flagstone path towards the impressive stone mansion that had been converted into a community home for young people struggling with life's problems. She and Daniel and the children lived in the smaller cottage that had once been the estate manager's home.

Through the fog, Lake Linnhe was barely visible, but the gentle lapping of the waves against the shore confirmed that the large body of water was indeed only a stone's throw away. As Lizzy approached the sturdy mansion covered in creeping ivy, and normally surrounded by a beautiful flower garden, she realised how much she would miss it, if and when they left. Not that anything was planned, but both she and Daniel had a sense that God was about to lead them onto something new.

Lizzy ducked around the side of the mansion and pushed open the heavy wooden door, the servants' entrance in years gone by, but now the entrance used mostly by the students. She made her way down the hallway, following the aroma of freshly baked bread all the way to the kitchen where her sister-in-law, Caitlin, was busy at work. She and Caitlin were spending the morning in the big kitchen, and had planned to bake lots of meals and treats in readiness for everyone's arrival.

Caitlin looked up as Lizzy entered, her round, jolly face lighting up. "Come and warm up, Liz. The teapot's still hot if you'd like a cuppa."

"Thanks. I'll grab one in a moment." Lizzy headed straight for the wood stove, holding her hands in front of it, and shivering again as warmth spread slowly from the tips of her fingers, up her arms, and into the rest of her body. She rubbed her hands together and glanced out the window where Ben Nevis, the tallest mountain in Great Britain, would normally be visible in the distance. "It's such a dreadful morning."

"You're not wrong. A great welcome for everyone." Chuckling, Caitlin opened a bag of onions, pulling several out.

Lizzy stepped away from the fire and poured herself a mug of tea. She lifted the pot in the air and looked at Caitlin. "Like a top-up?"

"No thanks, I'm on my third already. How long until everyone starts arriving?" Caitlin blew some hair off her face as she diced the onions for the shepherd's pie they'd decided to serve for dinner.

"Three hours, maybe less if the fog lifts." Lizzy cupped her hands around the mug and blew on her tea.

"The girls will be down in a minute." Caitlin looked up, brushing her watering eyes with her sleeve. "I almost forgot to tell you—Andrew also offered to help."

Lizzy rolled her eyes. "Wow, we'll need to be on our toes." Andrew, a chef at one of the top restaurants in Glasgow, and the son of David and Rosemary McKinnon, the owners of the property, had arrived the previous evening to spend Christmas with his parents.

"I think it'll be fun. I've always wanted to cook with a real chef."

"It's all right for you. I struggle just to do the basics." Lizzy took a sip of tea before placing the mug on the kitchen table and donning an apron, tying it securely behind her back.

"I'm sure it'll be fine, but you can work with the girls if you'd rather."

"I thought they might have gone to the airport with Daniel and Caleb?"

"No... twelve going on twenty. You know what it's like." Caitlin chuckled. "They spend hours in front of the mirror these days."

"They're lovely girls. You and Caleb have done a great job with them."

"Thanks. They're going to miss it here when we go back to Belfast." Caleb had been the Activities Co-ordinator at the community for the past several years, but the family was returning to Belfast because Caitlin's mother had taken ill.

"They must be looking forward to seeing their friends again."

"They'd rather be here with their new friends." Caitlin wiped her face again.

"They'll adjust quickly." Lizzy took out a mixing bowl and grabbed the ingredients to start making a triple-sized bread and butter pudding. With so many mouths to feed, they'd chosen easy to prepare meals they could make ahead of time.

"I hope so. It's a hard age to uproot them." Putting the knife down, Caitlin grabbed a handful of tissues and blew her nose.

"They can always come back for a visit."

"I'm sure they'd like that." Caitlin threw the tissues into the bin and washed her hands, then turned to the doorway, her face lighting up when Imogen and Tara, both wearing hot pink sweat shirts, dark blue jeans and black joggers, appeared. She held out her arm. "And here they are."

Lizzy chuckled. How could she still not tell them apart after almost two years? She gave them a smile. "Hi, girls. Are you excited about Christmas?"

The girls both nodded as they entered together and stood in front of the free-standing island bench where Caitlin had resumed dicing the onions.

"Cat got your tongue, girls? Answer your auntie."

One of them, maybe Imogen, turned and looked at Lizzy. Her eyes, although dark like her mother's, were innocent and clear. "Sorry, Auntie Lizzy. Yes, we're very much looking forward to Christmas."

Lizzy smiled. "My three certainly are. They can't wait. Every morning they check the tree for new presents."

Caitlin tipped the tray of onions into a large pan on the stove. "Come on, girls, you need to get to work. You're on vegetables."

"Mum..." Their shoulders slumped.

Caitlin stirred the onions as they began sizzling, filling the kitchen with a wonderful aroma. "Only joking. You can bake some gingerbread men and then help with the trifle."

The face of the twin who'd answered earlier lit up. "That's better. Come on, Tara, let's get started."

Lizzy smiled to herself. For once she'd guessed right!

Soon after, as Imogen and Tara were busy mixing dough for the gingerbread men and Lizzy buttered bread for the pudding, Andrew knocked on the door and poked his head in. "I believe this is where it's all happening. May I come in?" The words rolled off his tongue in a soft Scottish brogue.

Caitlin looked up. "Please do! We've been expecting you."

Andrew took the apron Caitlin offered him and slipped it on. As he rolled up his sleeves, Lizzy couldn't help but notice the curly ginger hair on his fair arms. With that tawny-gold hair with a hint of ginger, and his warm hazel eyes, Andrew McKinnon would be a great catch for someone, *if he were available.* Lizzy's mind ticked over. *Brianna?* She chuckled as she returned to her pudding. Yes, Brianna. It was time Daniel's younger sister had some love in her life, and the softly spoken, ruggedly handsome Andrew McKinnon would be her perfect match.

CHAPTER 2

*A*s Lizzy expected, her parents, Roger and Gwyneth Walton-Smythe from Wiveliscombe Manor in the south of England, arrived first. While she greeted them at the main door, a dark coloured SUV turned into the driveway and pulled up behind her parents' BMW. The front passenger door opened, and Grace, Daniel's sister who was closest to him in age, stepped out, her long legs easily reaching the ground as she quickly slipped on her dark red coat. Grace then opened the back door for her younger sister, Brianna, who, by the way she stretched, looked like she'd just woken up. Grace's husband, Ryan, lifted their cases out of the boot and followed the women to the main entrance.

Lizzy greeted everyone and made the introductions, and after they'd all removed and hung their coats, she ushered them into the drawing room. The log fire Andrew had lit earlier that morning crackled in the huge fireplace, the smell of pine needles filling the room with a reassuringly familiar smell.

Without Daniel and the children there, Lizzy wondered how the next hour or so would go, but she had nothing to worry about. Grace, as confident and charming as ever, engaged her mother in conversation, but Brianna headed straight for the kitchen. Although she had grown in confidence since kicking her drug habit and giving her heart to the Lord almost two years ago, there was no doubt she'd feel intimidated by Roger and Gwyneth. Lizzy's parents couldn't help the way they spoke, but she knew many considered them *posh*. It wouldn't worry Grace, who'd been a high-profile prosecuting barrister prior to her marriage to Ryan, but Brianna? A different matter altogether.

Lizzy sometimes wondered if Grace missed the challenge of the court room now that she was managing the "Place of Hope", the rape support and counselling centre she and Brianna had opened in Glasgow following Grace's acquittal of involvement in a terrorist attack. Seeing the way Grace and Ryan looked at each other, Lizzy decided that Grace was content with her new life, especially as she now had no secrets to hide and her slate had been wiped clean by the blood of Jesus.

Lizzy sat down and joined the conversation between her mother and Grace, while Ryan stood with his back to the fire and chatted with her father. Caitlin poked her head into the room. Despite her face being flushed from cooking, she still wore a cheery smile.

"Caitlin, come in and say hello." Lizzy held her hand out

and motioned for her to join them. "You remember my mother, Gwyneth?"

"Of course I do." Caitlin smoothed her hair and straightened her apron before stepping closer and taking Gwyneth's hand. Lizzy hoped Caitlin wouldn't curtsy and breathed a sigh of relief when she leaned down and placed a kiss on Gwyneth's cheek. "Nice to see you again, Gwyneth. How was your trip?"

Gwyneth smiled politely. "Not too bad, considering the weather and the time of year. We only came from Edinburgh this morning, so we didn't have far to come."

"No, but the fog was terrible, and it still hasn't lifted." Grace stood and gave Caitlin a hug. Tall and elegant as always, Grace towered over her short, pudgy sister-in-law. "How are you, Caitlin?"

"I'm fine, thanks. Good to see you, Grace." An easy smile played at the corners of Caitlin's mouth as she took Grace's hands in hers. There had been a time back in Belfast before Grace met the Lord when she barely acknowledged Caitlin's existence, but things had changed. God had transformed Grace's life so much that Lizzy still had to pinch herself occasionally to believe it had really happened.

Caitlin let go of Grace's hand. "Can I get everyone a drink before lunch?"

Gwyneth smiled. "A cup of tea would be lovely, thank you. I'm sure Roger would like one, too." She glanced at him, but his back was turned and he and Ryan were engrossed in conversation.

"I'll make a pot and bring it in." Caitlin took a step backwards towards the door, her head bobbing.

"I'll give you a hand." Lizzy went to stand.

"No, stay there. Brianna and Andrew can help." Caitlin's mouth twisted into an infectious grin as she motioned for Lizzy to remain where she was.

Lizzy suppressed a chuckle. It was happening already, and she hadn't done a thing...

∾

BRIANNA'S EYES had widened when she entered the kitchen. A man with the most gorgeous gingery golden hair stood at the sink washing dishes. She began back pedalling when Caitlin gestured for her to come in.

Jolly as always, and totally unaware of Brianna's hesitancy, Caitlin drew her into an embrace. "Great to see you, sweetheart. How are you doing?"

Brianna blinked, momentarily tearing her gaze from the man at the sink to return Caitlin's hug, but her gaze had a mind of its own and kept darting back to him. *Who is this man? And what's he doing standing at the sink, washing dishes, wearing an apron?* She blinked again and answered Caitlin's question, forcing herself to smile at her sister-in-law. "I'm good, glad to be having a break."

Caitlin held Brianna's gaze, her eyes smiling. "Danny will be pleased you're here."

Brianna sucked in a breath. "Yes, well, he owes me a trip to Spain."

Caitlin chuckled. "You never know with Danny; he might just surprise you. Anyway, come and meet Andrew, Rosemary and David's son."

Brianna's eyes widened again. *Of course...* Rosemary, the

owner of the property and the support person for the female students, had mentioned her son several times while Brianna had been a student at the community. Rosemary had even proudly shown her some family photos, but Brianna had taken little notice at the time. Now she wished she had. Caitlin grabbed her hand and drew her towards the most disturbingly attractive man she'd ever laid eyes on. As Andrew McKinnon turned around, Brianna's gaze was drawn to his hazel eyes, soft, warm, and dancing with amusement.

Brianna averted her gaze quickly, but it was too late. He'd seen her reaction. If only the floor would open up and swallow her now.

"Brianna, is it? Nice to meet you." Goose bumps ran over her skin as the soft Scottish inflections rolled off Andrew's tongue.

She was too surprised at her reaction to do more than nod, but she had to say something. She offered him a small, shy smile. "Yes, nice to meet you, too." Her throat was tight, her voice shaky.

Andrew extended his hand. Brianna reluctantly reached out and took it. As their skin touched, her flesh tingled. His hand, firm and strong, was surprisingly tender, like nothing she'd felt before. The nearness of this man overwhelmed her, and she quickly withdrew her hand and stepped back.

"Did I hear you were going to Spain?" He reached behind his back and undid the apron. As he removed it, Brianna took in his tall, athletic physique and tried to remember what Rosemary had said about him.

"Ah, ah... yes..." She was stuttering, but couldn't help

herself. "I… was going with a friend, but I cancelled because of the family gathering."

"You'd love Spain. You should go one day." Andrew hung the apron on a hook behind the door.

With his back turned, Brianna took the opportunity to get Caitlin's attention. She needed help, but Caitlin just grinned, her eyes glinting.

"I'm going to say hello to everyone. Can you make a pot of tea, Brianna? I'm sure they'll want one after their drive."

Brianna's eyes widened. What was Caitlin doing? Surely she wouldn't leave her here alone with Andrew? Caitlin knew she wasn't any good with men.

Caitlin didn't wait for an answer. She grinned mischievously and bustled from the kitchen.

Brianna's heart raced. Caitlin had given her no choice. She'd make the tea and try not to embarrass herself, and then she'd escape. Quickly grabbing the cannister of tea from the shelf beside the window, she heaped spoonsful of the black leaves into the tea pot.

"You know your way around this kitchen." Andrew leaned back against the bench with one ankle crossed over the other and his arms folded.

Brianna swallowed hard. She'd have to tell him she used to be a student here, but as soon as she did, she'd be giving Andrew a glimpse of her past. Only people with problems came to the community, and since his parents owned the place, he'd know that. She took a deep breath. What did it matter? God had healed her deep inside, but it was still hard talking about her past, especially with such a disturbingly handsome man. But it would come out eventually. Rosemary would no doubt say something, so she may as well get it over with.

She plopped another spoonful of tea into the pot and kept her head down. "I used to be a student here."

He angled his head. "Really?"

Brianna wasn't sure if her answer had surprised him or not, but the tone of his voice suggested it hadn't. She nodded. "Yes, a couple of years ago."

"You'd know my mum, then."

Brianna looked up and smiled. Her heart warmed every time she thought of the kindly Scottish woman who'd taken her under her wing on the day she arrived. "Yes, your mum helped me so much."

"She's a special lady." Andrew picked up the large kettle whistling on the stove and poured the steaming water into the teapot.

Brianna was acutely aware of his masculine body and cologne as he stood near her filling the pot. His closeness was both confronting and disturbing. She breathed a sigh of relief when Caitlin returned.

"They all would like tea. Andrew, would you mind taking the tray in with the cups and saucers? Will you be okay with the pot, Brianna? I'm going to call the girls."

"I'll be fine." Brianna forced a smile. Caitlin was putting her on the spot, and she knew it. What if she spilled the tea on Lizzy's mother? And Grace would notice her unease straight away. She'd poured tea hundreds of times before, *but never with a man like Andrew McKinnon by my side.*

~

LIZZY GLANCED up as Brianna entered the drawing room. Looking uneasy, she carried the tea pot covered with a brightly coloured tea cosy, but Andrew, hot on her heels and wearing a wide grin, appeared to be enjoying himself.

"Thanks Brianna, Andrew. Just put it on the side board. I can pour." Lizzy stood, and after they'd placed the tray and pot down, gestured for them to join her. "Andrew, come and meet everyone." Lizzy made the introductions, and then, after they'd all exchanged pleasantries, she took orders. Andrew joined Ryan and her father in front of the fire, and Brianna helped distribute the cups of tea as Lizzy poured.

As Lizzy poured the last cup, Caitlin and the girls joined them, and everyone continued chatting while sipping tea and nibbling shortbread, but Lizzy kept an amused eye on Brianna and Andrew. Sparks were flying between them, and it gladdened her heart. It was beyond time Brianna had someone special in her life, but it would challenge her. In Brianna's entire thirty-four years, she was yet to have a proper relationship with a man. Raped by her cousins at age fifteen, and losing her baby at age sixteen, Brianna had turned to drugs. Jesus had since healed her, but she would need God's grace and strength to get close to a man. But from what Lizzy had seen of Andrew McKinnon, she was convinced he was perfect for her. With his mother's gentle spirit and his own zest for life, Andrew McKinnon could be exactly what Brianna needed. *But what if he already had someone special in his life?* She'd just have to pray he didn't.

After a short while, Lizzy suggested everyone freshen up before lunch. She showed her parents to the upstairs room. Normally her parents stayed in the cottage, but Daniel had thought it would be fun for them all to stay in the big house, so Lizzy had prepared a room for her parents in the east wing, where she, Daniel, and the children would also stay.

As they climbed the spiral wooden staircase, Lizzy turned her head and smiled at her parents. "I'm glad you were able to make it. The children can't wait to see you. In fact, they should be here any minute." She glanced at her watch. *Where were they?*

Gwyneth's expression grew wistful. "It's a pity your brother couldn't make it. One of these years we'll spend Christmas all together."

"I haven't seen Jonathon since he visited briefly last year. He seems to just do his own thing, or at least that's the impression I got."

"He's so caught up in his world, I don't think anything else matters to him anymore. Especially family."

Lizzy slipped her arm around her mother's slim waist. "Don't worry, Mum, you've got us."

"Yes, but look how far away you live."

Lizzy sighed. Her mother was right, they did live a long way apart, and as much as she loved the ruggedness of the Highlands and being involved in the community, she missed being close to her parents. Surprising, really, after all the years when she and her father could barely share a civilised word. But things had changed so much, and her father now didn't just approve of Daniel, he loved him. "Let's not think about that now."

Lizzy paused at the top of the stairs where the bunch of fresh flowers she'd bought at the local florist the day before sat on a highly polished timber dresser.

Her mother's gaze swept over the large room the students

used as a lounge area. A bookcase, overflowing with books of all sorts, filled one wall, and an old piano another. Three oversized couches, covered with lap rugs and brightly coloured cushions, faced a large open-fireplace. A large coffee table sat in the centre. Lizzy had tidied the pile of magazines the students had left behind, and they now sat neatly on one corner of the table. Board games were piled on another, and in the middle, a smaller bunch of fresh flowers.

"This is very cosy," Gwyneth said approvingly.

"I'd forgotten you hadn't been up here before. I'll have to give you a tour, or maybe Rosemary can."

"I'd like that."

"Your room's down this way." Lizzy motioned to her left and led her parents down a long hallway lit with old-fashioned wall sconces and decorated with oil paintings and tapestries, stopping outside a door on her right which she held open for them to enter. "I hope you'll be comfortable here."

As her mother stepped inside the large guest room, her gaze travelled around the best room in the house. Lizzy had made sure everything was perfect... her parents liked nice things, and so she had gone shopping and bought an expensive, high quality duvet cover, matching pillow cases and new fluffy towels. She'd even contemplated updating the long, slightly faded drapes, but that would have been going too far. "It looks wonderful, doesn't it, Roger?" Gwyneth slipped her hand into the crook of her husband's arm and looked at his face.

Although he gave her a warm smile, he still stood rigidly. "Perfect. Thank you, Elizabeth."

Lizzy stifled a chuckle. When would her father give in and

shorten her name like everyone else did? "Great. Let me know if you need anything."

Gwyneth grabbed Lizzy's hand, her eyes moistening. "Thank you, dear. It really is good to see you."

Lizzy stepped forward and gave her mother a big hug. "And it's good to see you, Mum. I'm sorry it's been so long."

Soon after, as Lizzy left her parents to freshen up, she checked her watch again and tried to ignore the lump growing in the pit of her stomach. *Where are they?* Daniel had called when he and Caleb arrived at the airport, but that was hours ago. She blew out a breath and hurried down the steps. *God, please keep them safe, wherever they are...*

CHAPTER 3

*D*aniel and Caleb and the children arrived at Inverness Airport half an hour later than planned due to the heavy fog, and were relieved to discover that the plane carrying their siblings from Belfast had also been delayed and had only just landed. They waited in the Arrivals Hall for another half an hour before the group of six emerged.

Aislin clutched her husband's hand. Alana held three-year-old Quinn's hand, and Shawn and Brendan, looking like body guards, brought up the rear. As they wandered out, their eyes scanned the crowd.

Daniel drew a breath and sent up a quick prayer. *God, please bless our time together...*

Each of his siblings had their own unique stories, but none, apart from Aislin and Alana, who'd lived together for most of their lives until Aislin had recently married her long-time boyfriend, Joel, really knew each other. Shawn was a mystery to them all, having travelled the world for most of his adult life, rarely returning to Belfast. It was a miracle he was home and had agreed to join the family for Christmas. It was also a miracle Brendan was out of jail. How would these two in particular cope with staying at a Christian community? Would they feel uncomfortable? Would there be arguments and disagreements? How much of the past would be raked through? What would these four, plus Joel, think about the other four siblings, including himself, who'd given their hearts to the Lord? Would they consider them soft and weak?

Daniel had asked God to bless their time together and trusted He'd smooth the way, but had he been too ambitious? He released his breath and raised his hand, catching Brendan's eye. Brendan nodded in acknowledgment, but his expression remained unchanged. Daniel gulped. What had he gotten himself into? Brendan was a hardened criminal who mixed with other hardened criminals, yet when he attended Da's funeral several years ago, he had a tear in his eye as the coffin was lowered into the ground. There was hope for even the toughest of criminals—no one was beyond God's saving grace, and didn't Daniel know that.

He shifted Clare to his other hip and pushed his way through the crowd. Caleb held James' hand and followed closely behind. Seven-year-old Dillon raced ahead, darting around groups of people and stopping only when Daniel called out.

The men shook hands, Daniel and Caleb kissed and hugged the girls, and Quinn clung to his mother, studying everyone with big, round eyes covered by lashes too long for a boy.

"Welcome to Scotland, everyone. Great to see you all.

Thanks for coming." Daniel spoke too fast, and his chest was tight.

Caleb clapped Daniel on the back and stood beside him. "It means a lot to both of us that you've come. It really is great to see you all."

Alana's eyes misted over. She quickly wiped them with the back of her hand and pulled Quinn tighter.

Aislin smiled. "We're all glad to be here, aren't we?" Clinging to Joel's arm, she glanced at each of her siblings in turn, urging them to agree.

Brendan looked down at his shoes before raising his head, his expression softening. "Yeah, I'm glad to be here."

"I am too, I think." Shawn stood with his hands in the pockets of his red bomber jacket. Despite his years of travelling, he hadn't lost his Irish accent.

Alana just nodded. Black streaks from tears mixed with mascara ran down her cheeks.

Daniel gave her an extra hug, but if he made too much of a fuss, he too could end up in tears.

Caleb rubbed his hands together. "We'd better get moving. The fog's started to lift, but it'll still take about two hours to get home." He headed for the exit and everyone followed.

Daniel unlocked the twenty-seater community bus, and after he and Caleb stacked the suitcases in the back, they ushered everyone into their seats. Clare clung to him, wanting to sit beside him in the front. He probably should have left her at home with Lizzy, but she'd been excited to come. It was a different story now... not surprising, really. Brendan and Shawn would intimidate anyone.

"It's okay, Danny. I'll sit in the back." Caleb knew what it was like to have a shy daughter. He had two.

"Thanks, man, appreciate it."

Daniel's hopes for a drive home filled with happy chatter soon flew out the window. Engaging everyone in conversation was hard work, a lot harder than he'd expected. Aislin and Joel chatted on and off with Caleb, as did Shawn, but Brendan and Alana barely said a word. And he had to concentrate on the road.

At just under the half-way mark, when the crumbly remains of Urquhart Castle and the deep, dark waters of Loch Ness came into view on their left, Daniel rounded a corner and slammed on the brakes. A truck on its side blocked the road. The bus skidded and fish-tailed. Clare screamed. Daniel pressed harder, trying to bring it to a stop. A deathly hush filled the back of the bus. The bus stopped inches from the truck. Daniel blew out a deep breath and reached for Clare, pulling her close, comforting her, and very glad she'd been wearing a seat belt. He turned around and cast his gaze over the rest of his passengers. "Is everyone okay?"

One by one they either nodded or said quietly that they were, but all their faces were pale. He thanked God silently that no one had been hurt, but then his thoughts turned to the driver of the truck. "Clare, Daddy and Uncle Caleb have to go outside and look at the truck. Can you climb into the back with your aunties?"

"I want to stay with you, Daddy." She shot several quick glances into the back but then buried her head in Daniel's shoulder.

He gently pried her head up and looked into her eyes,

wiping her damp face with his fingers. "I know, sweetheart, but it's cold outside, and I won't be long. Will you do it for me?"

Looking at him with a serious expression, she nodded. "Okay, but come back quickly."

"I will, sweetheart. Thank you." He hugged her and then helped her climb over the centre console into the back. Aislin reached out and lifted her onto the seat beside her that Joel had just vacated. Joel, Caleb, Shawn and Brendan had already jumped out and were sprinting to the truck. Daniel quickly reversed the bus away from the wreck, switched on the warning lights, and then followed them, pulling his beanie over his ears as a blast of icy wind hit him.

Approaching the truck, which lay on its side, Daniel wondered what they would find. Many years ago, when he and Lizzy had just met, he was an orderly at a hospital and had seen many traffic accident victims wheeled in with various degrees of injury, and he and Caleb had both taken emergency first-aid courses as part of their jobs at the community, but even with all that preparation and training, dread filled him. He prayed the driver had survived, but held little hope as the cab had almost completely crumpled when it hit the stone wall bordering the road.

As more people stopped at the accident, the potential danger grew. Steam hissed from the engine, and there was every possibility the truck could burst into flames any second. It was too dangerous for any of them to go inside, but Caleb and Brendan had already scaled the crumpled side and were on top. A sinking feeling, like being swept out to sea in an ebbing tide, flowed through him.

He took a moment to catch his breath as he reached Joel

and Shawn who were holding people back on the other side of the truck. "Has anybody called emergency services?"

"Someone drove back to that town we just passed to make the call," Joel replied.

Daniel ran his hand over his beanie. "It'll be at least half an hour before any services can get here, if not longer. Do we know if the driver's okay?"

"Not yet. They just got up there." Joel glanced to the top of the cab where Caleb and Brendan had been moments earlier, but were no longer in sight.

"I'll go and help." As Daniel moved closer to the truck, Joel grabbed him.

"It's too dangerous, stay here. They'll call if they need help."

Daniel paused. Joel was right. What if the truck exploded? Caleb and Brendan were risking their lives up there. He prayed for their safety and returned to stand with the others. At least there wasn't another vehicle involved. He looked at the road and scratched his head. How had it happened? *Must have been speed.* But why would a local carrier, who knew the road and the conditions, speed along here, especially with visibility so low? *Crazy.*

A bang made them all jump. Daniel's heart thudded. *Oh God, please keep Caleb safe.* What would he say to Caitlin and the girls if Caleb didn't make it home? No, that wasn't going to happen. He rushed forward and started climbing. "Caleb, get out of there. It's not safe."

"He's alive, Danny. We've got to get him out." Caleb's voice was desperate.

Daniel bit his lip and continued climbing as another bang split the air. "I'm coming up." He clambered up the wrecked metal, grabbing hold of whatever he could until he reached the top and then peered in through the smashed window.

"Danny, help us get him out. Grab his head and shoulders and we'll support his body." Caleb's face, smeared with blood, wore determination like Daniel had never seen.

"Okay, let's do this." Daniel manoeuvered himself into a better position. As Caleb and Brendan carefully lifted the man up, he bore the weight of the man's upper torso until his whole body was clear. Daniel yelled down to where everyone stood. "Joel, Shawn, come and help."

The two men raced over and took the weight of the man from Daniel as Caleb and Brendan clambered out of the smashed-up cab. They laid him onto a patch of grass beside the loch moments before the truck exploded.

Daniel gazed in awe at the fireball and thanked God for His perfect timing before returning his focus to the man. His face paled. He knew him. Fraser McAdams. He lived in Fort William and his wife, Niamh, was due to give birth any day. *That's why he was speeding.* Fraser must have gotten word she was ready to deliver. "Okay, let's have some room. Is there a doctor here?"

Everyone in the gathered crowd looked at each other, but no one came forward. "What about a nurse?" Still no one stepped up. Daniel met Caleb's gaze. "Looks like it's you and me."

"We can do this." Caleb knelt down on the opposite side of the man and lowered his face. "Fraser, can you hear me?"

Fraser moaned.

"Where does it hurt?"

Fraser groaned louder.

Caleb glanced up at Daniel, the muscles in his neck taut. "We need to check his airways."

Daniel carefully tilted Fraser's head back, opened his mouth and peered inside. "Clear."

"We need to make him comfortable and stop that bleed." Caleb raised Fraser's bloodied shirt and gagged. He lowered the shirt and then looked at the crowd. "Has anyone got a towel?" His voice was desperate as he held his hands tightly over the oozing wound.

"I have," someone called out. "I'll get it."

Moments later, the person handed Daniel a towel which he folded quickly into a pad and carefully slipped under Caleb's hands to stanch the bleeding. Daniel kept pressure on the wound and prayed. Fraser couldn't bleed to death. Niamh would be devastated. Minutes ticked by until sirens sounded in the distance. Daniel breathed a sigh of relief.

A fire engine and an ambulance arrived at the same time, followed closely by a tow truck. The paramedics took over but praised Daniel and Caleb for their swift actions which most likely saved Fraser's life. They lifted him onto a stretcher and into the ambulance and whisked him off to the hospital. The fire fighters took another twenty minutes to fully extinguish the blaze, and it took two tow trucks almost an hour to right the wrecked vehicle and get it onto one of them before the road was re-opened.

Almost two hours after their trip was interrupted, the men headed back to the bus to re-join Aislin, Alana and the children, who were huddled together with blankets wrapped around them watching the proceedings from a safe distance.

Clare ran towards Daniel. When she stopped, she looked up

at him, her eyes big, round and full of concern. "Will the man be okay, Daddy?"

His heart melted. Bending down, he rested one knee on the ground to level his face with hers. "Yes, sweetheart. The doctors will fix him and make him better."

"Can we ask God to help, too?"

"That's a great idea. Shall we do that now?"

Clare nodded, thumb in mouth.

"Would you like to pray?"

"Okay." As Clare bowed her head, Daniel placed his hand on her shoulder to steady himself and then bowed his head, too. Clare's little voice was so sweet. "Dear God, please help the man get better before Christmas so he can be home with his family when Santa comes. Thank you that Daddy was able to help him. Amen."

Daniel added his own request. "And dear God, please be with the man's wife as she brings their new little baby into the world."

Clare's head shot up. "Are they getting a baby for Christmas?"

Daniel laughed. "You could say that."

"Can we get a baby for Christmas, too?"

"Not this year, sweetheart."

"Next year?"

"Maybe." Standing, he ruffled her hair and took her hand. "We need to go home now. Mummy will be wondering where we are."

"Okay." She smiled sweetly as they walked back to the others.

"Would you like me to drive?" Shawn asked as Daniel approached.

"That would be super, thanks." Clapping him on the back, Daniel gave him a grateful smile.

Brendan joined Shawn in the front, while Daniel joined the children in the back. He wasn't sure what had happened, but everyone seemed closer. Maybe witnessing such a terrible accident had made them appreciate their own lives and family more than before. Whatever it was, he felt blessed to be surrounded by his family, and thanked God for bringing them all together.

CHAPTER 4

When the bus pulled up outside the main building, Lizzy dashed outside with Caitlin right behind her. They'd heard about the accident near the castle on the news and figured Daniel and Caleb and the others had been caught up in it. Everyone back at the community had been relieved it was a truck, and not a bus that had crashed, and then immediately Lizzy and Caitlin felt guilty. When they heard the injured man was Fraser McAdams, they felt even worse. His wife, Niamh, belonged to their Wednesday Bible study group, and they'd heard she was in the early stages of labour. They'd all gathered together and prayed for both her and Fraser, and had been waiting eagerly for Daniel and Caleb to return with the rest of the family.

As Daniel climbed out of the side door of the bus with Clare's arms wrapped around his neck, Lizzy's heart filled with gratitude—it could so easily have been them. She quickly closed the gap between them and threw her arms around

Daniel. He reeked of smoke, grease and dried blood, but she didn't care. She held him close and pushed back the tears stinging her eyes. "Thank God you're all safe. We were so worried." She leaned into his chest before pulling back and looking into his eyes. "Will Fraser be all right?"

"We prayed for him, Mummy." Clare reached out and twiddled a strand of Lizzy's hair.

"That's wonderful, Clare. I'm sure God will look after him."

"And Daddy said they're getting a baby for Christmas!"

Lizzy fought the urge to laugh. "Yes, they *are* getting a baby for Christmas. Let's pray Fraser will be home before it comes."

"Is Santa bringing it?"

Lizzy gently shook her head as she touched Clare's cheek. "Not really, but let's talk about that later, okay?"

"Okay."

She and Daniel had debated about whether to tell the children the truth about Santa or not, but hadn't been able to agree. He couldn't see the harm in letting the children find out in their own time, but Lizzy wanted to tell them, and moments like this just confirmed to her they should.

Daniel kissed the top of her head and then eased himself from her arms. "Everyone's okay, love, that's the main thing. And we've got guests to think of now."

He was right. They could have this conversation later. She smiled into his eyes and then turned to greet the family. After everyone hugged and kissed, she and Daniel led them inside and introduced her parents to the family from Ireland. Grace and Brianna hugged their brothers and sisters, and then everyone sat down for a cup of tea and a chat.

Lizzy kept an amused eye on Brianna and Andrew. Brianna

sat on the couch beside Aislin and Alana, but every now and then she shot a coy glance at Andrew, who was talking with Ryan, Brendan, Shawn and Daniel. And every now and then, Andrew shot a glance at her, but their eyes never met. Maybe they needed a little help after all. She'd sit them together tonight at dinner.

After everyone had finished their tea, Caitlin and Lizzy took the new arrivals upstairs and settled them into their rooms. Lizzy wondered how Brendan and Shawn would cope living so close to everyone, but then, these accommodations would be luxury compared to a jail cell, and Shawn would be used to bunking down with others, so she quickly put her concerns to rest.

She excused herself after a while. Daniel had taken the children to their rooms, and although he was more than capable of looking after them, she wanted to make sure they were all okay after witnessing the accident. "Feel free to take a wander around, have a rest, whatever you like. Dinner will be at six in the main dining area. Call out if you need anything before then."

"We'll be fine, Lizzy. We're all big people and can look after ourselves." Grace said, lifting her gaze from the magazine she'd been flicking through as she sat on one of the couches in front of the fire. She leaned against Ryan with her long legs elegantly crossed on the coffee table.

Lizzy laughed. Grace would never have done that in her fancy apartment. How far she'd come to be so relaxed. "I know, I'm sorry. We just want everyone to have a nice time."

"And we will. Off you go and look after your family." Grace dismissed her with a wave of her hand and a playful grin.

"Thank you." Lizzy chuckled as she headed down the hallway with a plate of freshly baked gingerbread men to where the laughter and giggles of happy children, *and Daniel*, spilled out of the room next to her parents. Hopefully putting them so close wasn't a mistake.

～

BRIANNA WAS SHARING a room with Alana and Quinn. That morning, when she'd arrived with Grace and Ryan, Lizzy had asked if she minded staying in her old room, the room she'd shared with Susan and Maggie when she'd arrived at Elim Community as a suicidal drug addict more than two years ago. The room hadn't changed a bit. It was still as cozy and lovely as it had been on the day she first saw it, and the view of the mountains, still shrouded in mist, took her breath away. Living in the city, she missed the mountains—she'd never thought she would, but there was something special about them… calming, yet at the same time, awe-inspiring. Brianna had already unpacked, and now she sat on the chair with Quinn on her lap while Alana unpacked.

She hardly knew Alana. When all the siblings had been separated after Mam died, Brianna and Grace, ages ten and twelve, were sent to Londonderry to stay with Aunt Hilda, but Aislin and Alana, the two youngest girls, stayed in Belfast with another aunt and uncle. Now, more than twenty years later, they were both adults. Brianna looked at her younger sister and saw a lifetime of sadness in her eyes. Working with rape victims every day, Brianna had come to know a lot about the human heart, and how if someone said they were okay, often

38

their eyes told a different story. Alana may not have been raped, but she was hurting, and Brianna's heart wept for her. Maybe God had put them together so she could share God's love with Alana, just like Rosemary had shared His love with her not that not long ago in this very room.

Brianna pulled Quinn closer. Holding him made her think of her own little son who'd died when he was only two months old. Even after all this time, she still felt the pain of loss, but it wasn't as fresh anymore. God had healed the bitterness and hurt she'd carried for many years, but if she wanted Alana to feel comfortable with her, Brianna had to earn her trust, and as painful as it might be, sharing the part of her life that Alana would relate to might help.

"Quinn's a beautiful little boy. You must be proud of him." Brianna's smile shifted from him to Alana.

Alana looked up from her suitcase, her face splitting into a wide grin. "He's the best thing that's happened in my life."

"I had a son..." Brianna's smile slipped as she took a slow breath.

Alana angled her head, her forehead creasing. "I didn't know that. What happened to him?"

Brianna's tears were just below the surface as the memory of her beautiful little boy returned. "Aedan died of pneumonia when he was two months old."

Alana sat on the bed and lifted her gaze. "I'm sorry. That must have been horrible."

"It was a long time ago, but yes, it was." Brianna closed her eyes for a moment, remembering the last time she held Aedan, just moments before he died.

"Were you ..." Alana's voice trailed away.

Brianna grimaced. "Raped?" She mouthed the word so Quinn wouldn't hear it.

Alana nodded, her eyes wide.

"How did you know?"

Alana shrugged and looked down at her hands, fidgeting with them. "I kind of guessed, you working at that Rape Centre and all." She looked up, her eyes sad.

Brianna released a deep sigh. "It was all such a long time ago, and I try not to think about it much, although it's hard not to, considering where I work."

"I don't know what I'd do if I lost Quinn." Alana reached out and squeezed Quinn's hand, her eyes moistening.

"What happened to his father?" It was a risk asking, but if Alana didn't want to talk, that was fine.

She lowered her gaze and picked at her nails. "He left when I was seven months pregnant. He said being a father scared him." She raised her head. "Being a mother scared me to bits, but I didn't have a choice. I thought he was excited about having a baby. He was at the beginning. We'd been together for a long time. I obviously didn't know him as well as I thought I did."

"Where is he now?"

Tears filled Alana's eyes. "Living with some chick on the other side of the city."

Brianna quickly moved beside Alana and wrapped an arm around her shoulder, pulling her close. Quinn wriggled onto the floor and stood in front of his mother, looking up at her with enlarged eyes.

Alana reached out, and sitting him on her lap, pulled him close. "I love you, Quinny. Mummy's okay. Don't worry." As she rocked him and kissed the top of his dark, wavy hair, her voice choked.

Brianna prayed silently for them as she held Alana tight. *Dear Lord, please help me show Your love to Alana and Quinn. She's hurting so much. Please help her open her heart to You this Christmas, dear Lord, and give her new life full of hope and peace. Please bless her, dear Lord.* Brianna wiped her eyes, and straightening, she rubbed Alana's back and put on a happy face. "Come on, I'll help you unpack, and then maybe we can take a walk now the fog's lifted."

Alana brushed her eyes with the back of her hand and nodded. "I'd like that."

Shortly after, dressed in warm coats and walking boots, Brianna, Alana and Quinn headed outside. The top of Ben Nevis was still covered in low-lying clouds, but the sky had cleared to a pale blue, and the sun, although low on the horizon, shone weakly on Loch Linnhe, drawing them to the water's edge. Several row boats, tied securely to the jetty, bobbed up and down in the gentle waves, making a splashing noise.

Quinn's face lit up. "Can we go for a ride?"

"It's a bit too cold, Quinny. Maybe tomorrow," Alana replied.

Quinn's little face fell and his bottom lip protruded in a pout. "I'm not cold."

Alana laughed. "Yes, you are. Your lips are blue and they're quivering."

"I think we need to play chasings to warm up," Brianna said as she began to run. "I bet you can't catch me," she called over her shoulder.

Quinn let go of Alana's hand and chased after Brianna, giggling when he caught her.

Brianna laughed. "You're such a fast runner. Okay, let's see if we can catch you."

Quinn took off, squealing and laughing. Within moments, Dillon and James came racing down from the big house. "Can we play too?" Dillon called out.

"Sure." Brianna stopped and pressed her hand to her chest. She'd just caught her breath when she felt, rather than heard, footsteps stop behind her. Her heart thumped. Somehow, she knew who it was—or did she just hope it was Andrew?

"Mind if I join in?" His voice held a trace of laughter and sent a tingle down her spine.

Her heart pounded, but not from running. She turned around and met Andrew's twinkling eyes. "Sure. You can be it." She tore her gaze away and called out to the children. "Hey, everyone, Andrew's it. See if you can catch him."

Andrew's athleticism amazed Brianna. He dodged James and Quinn, and outran Dillon. He laughed when she tried to catch hold of his coat as he zipped past, teasing her. Alana was the clever one, waiting for him to turn his back before leaping towards him and slapping him on the back.

It heartened Brianna to see Alana join in. The fresh, crisp air of the Highlands would do her good, just as it had done her not that long ago.

After a few more turns, they all collapsed onto the damp grass and caught their breath, but within minutes, the children wandered down to the edge of the loch.

"Don't get your boots wet, Quinny," Alana called out.

"You either, Dillon and James," Brianna called as loudly as she could.

Andrew chuckled. "Leave them be... they're boys."

"Yes, but they can still get sick." Brianna turned her head and met his gaze. Her pulse quickened.

"They'll be fine... leave them be." His gaze locked on hers.

She gulped. She'd never expected a man to affect her like this. Could she open her heart just a little and see what might happen? She'd witnessed both good and bad relationships. More bad than good if she were honest, but Danny and Lizzy, Caleb and Caitlin, and Grace and Ryan were all happy. Could she dare hope that she might also find happiness and love? Was it asking too much?

Brianna drew her gaze away and focused on the boys sploshing in the mud. There was only one way to find out, but the thought scared her to death. She'd convinced herself she would never get close to any man—it wasn't worth the risk. But now? Did she dare let her guard down just a fraction and see what might eventuate? The thought both thrilled and terrified her.

CHAPTER 5

*B*rianna's long wavy hair, bouncing softly on her shoulders, mesmerized Andrew as she walked ahead of him into the dining room that evening, but he couldn't stop his gaze drifting to her shapely figure. Snug plaid trousers and a cream cashmere sweater accentuated not only the brilliance of her hair, but her very attractive figure. He inhaled her sweet perfume wafting in the air, but then pulled himself up. Brianna was gorgeous, but he couldn't fall for her. What was he thinking? He had far greater things to deal with right now... but maybe it wouldn't hurt to spend a little time with her. She seemed different from the shallow, vain girls he mixed with—a downfall of his job. Apart from her looks, her fragility and tenderness attracted him. There was depth to Brianna O'Connor. If nothing else, she could be a good friend.

Brianna's eyes widened as he darted ahead and pulled the heavy wooden chair out for her. She gave him a shy nod and thanked him demurely. When she sat, she looked straight ahead with her hands folded in her lap. Her sister, Grace, and brother-in-law, Ryan, took the seats opposite. Her brother, Shawn, sat on Andrew's left. Andrew smiled when his parents took the seats beside Lizzy's parents at the top end of the long table.

He could easily feel like a gate-crasher. When he agreed to spend Christmas with his folks, he hadn't realised it actually meant spending it with the O'Connor family as well, but at least he'd have time to think. *And pray.* He released a sigh and pulled his thoughts back to the present. Time enough for that later.

Grace began chatting with Brianna, asking her about her afternoon. Grace, with hair much darker than Brianna's, was also a looker, but she was classy, sophisticated. Andrew had heard she'd been a lawyer. He was just about to join their conversation when Ryan caught his eye. "What do you do for a living, Andrew?" Ryan asked.

Andrew tore his attention from Brianna and Grace and answered Ryan. Before long, Ryan drew Shawn into the conversation, and within moments, they were chatting like best friends, especially when Andrew discovered both men had also travelled extensively.

Soon after, Brianna's older brother, Daniel stood at the head of the table and dinged a glass. "Can I have everyone's attention, please?"

Hush fell around the table as everyone turned their attention to him. He flashed an engaging smile as he cleared his throat. "I'd like to officially welcome you all. It's fantastic you could all come, and Lizzy and I are really looking forward to spending time with every one of you. Christmas is a season of celebration, and I'm so glad we can finally celebrate it together after all these years. Without any more ado, let's give thanks for this wonderful meal that my beautiful wife and sister-in-law have prepared." Daniel slipped his hand onto Lizzy's shoulder, sharing a smile with her before bowing his head to pray.

Andrew felt, rather than saw, Shawn shift uncomfortably in his seat. Giving thanks obviously wasn't something he was used to. Andrew could understand that. Although his parents were devout Christians, for many years he'd rejected the message of the gospel and felt uncomfortable when anyone gave thanks at the meal table. Shawn and the others would get plenty of that here. He hoped they'd cope, and that maybe their hearts might open a little to God's love over this festive period.

Once Daniel finished praying, Lizzy and Caitlin stood and headed for the kitchen. Andrew excused himself and joined them, reappearing moments later with trays of the shepherd's pie and vegetables they'd prepared that morning, placing the dishes at intervals along the table.

"Please help yourselves," Lizzy said as she placed a steaming dish of the pie in front of her parents.

Retaking his seat, Andrew picked up the server and cast his gaze around those nearby. "Can I dish out for everyone?"

Grace chuckled as she held her plate out. "You can be my mother any day."

He laughed. Surely she wasn't flirting? He scooped a medium-sized portion from the dish and placed it carefully onto her plate. "More?"

A mischievous grin brightened Grace's face. "Thank you, that's plenty."

Andrew then turned to Brianna. When their eyes met his

heart-rate increased, and for a moment, he forgot to speak, her eyes mesmerising him until she averted her gaze. He blinked and shifted in his seat. "Can I dish up for you, too, Brianna?" He spoke softly.

Lifting her gaze, she gave him another shy smile and held up her plate. "Yes, please."

As he spooned a similar-sized portion onto her plate, he stole a glance at her full mouth and her long, slender neck. She was truly beautiful. He cleared his throat. "Is that enough?"

"Yes, thank you." Her eyes lingered on his for a moment before she lowered them, her long, dark eyelashes fluttering.

He continued serving, but Brianna's delicate features were indelibly imprinted in his mind. When he finished serving everyone else, Andrew served himself and then paused before he began eating. All around him, chatter continued as people interspersed eating with talking. Ryan and Shawn discussed Shawn's adventures in Africa, and Grace talked with Brianna and Alana, seated on Brianna's other side, about recent happenings in Belfast. He tried listening to both conversations, but ended up chatting with the men. Just being near Brianna was enough. For now.

∼

LATER, following dessert, Brianna offered to help with the dishes on the off-chance that Andrew might offer his help as well. All through dinner she'd been wanting to talk with him, but didn't know how. She stood and began collecting the dirty dishes, her heart racing when he did the same. Grace and Ryan followed them to the kitchen, loaded with dirty dessert bowls and coffee mugs. The others adjourned to the main lounge area while Lizzy and Alana put the younger children to bed.

Brianna stacked the dishes ready for washing as Andrew filled one of the sinks with water. His nearness made her senses spin... she could easily drop the dishes if she wasn't careful.

"Tell me about yourself," Andrew said, as his eyes, gentle and soft, found hers.

Brianna laughed nervously, averting her gaze. "There's not much to tell."

His mouth tipped in a smile as he thrust his hands into the hot water. "I'm sure there is."

She blew out a frustrated breath, annoyed with herself. Grace and Ryan were chatting together at the other sink, and she'd gotten what she wanted—the chance to talk with Andrew. She talked easily with the women who came into the Rape Centre, but something about this man left her tongue-tied. It was silly. She had to pull herself together. Another opportunity like this might never come along. "You're right, but I don't know where to start." She grabbed a tea-towel and began wiping the dishes.

Andrew paused for a moment and looked at her with kind, understanding eyes. "Well, tell me where you live and what you do. That's a good place to start."

His easy-going manner relaxed her a little. The first question she could answer, but the second? Brianna swallowed hard and decided not to be embarrassed about what she did. Why should she be? He already knew she'd been a student here. "Okay, then. I live in Glasgow with a girlfriend, Susan. She was the one I was going to Spain with."

"How long have you lived in Glasgow?" His soft Scottish burr calmed her, but her gaze settled on his arms. Elbow high in water, ginger hairs glistened on his fair skin like gold sparkling in sunlight. She blinked and lifted her gaze. "Going on three years. Ever since I left the community."

"And what do you do in Glasgow?"

Brianna stiffened. It was the question she'd been dreading. Inhaling slowly, she picked up another bowl and began wiping it. "I work with Grace at a support centre called the Place of Hope."

"Really? With Grace?" His head tilted.

"Yes, with Grace. We started the centre when I left here." She paused. "It's a Rape Support Centre." Brianna held her breath while she waited for Andrew's reaction.

He didn't flinch. He just looked at her, eyes soft. "I wasn't expecting that. It must be a hard job."

Brianna released her breath and nodded. "We see some really sad cases."

He stopped washing and leaned back against the sink, drying his arms before folding them. "How do you manage?" His tone, filled with awe, surprised her further. But then, she shouldn't have been surprised—Rosemary had the same caring, gentle nature.

"I try not to bring it home, but it's hard not to. Some of the stories just stay with you, it doesn't matter what you do." She shrugged, trying not to meet his gaze, hoping he wouldn't ask the obvious question.

"I can understand that."

"I pray for them all, and I do things to get my mind off it. We try to take a break every few weeks. Grace makes sure we do that." Brianna let out a small, nervous chuckle as she glanced at her sister.

"Where do you go?"

"Mainly here to visit Danny and Lizzy." Brianna picked up another dish and held his gaze. "So now it's your turn. Tell me about you."

Andrew's face flickered before a playful grin lifted the corners of his mouth. "I wondered when we'd get to that." He turned back to the sink, but his voice had grown serious. Was he hiding something?

Brianna studied his back. "I should have made you go first."

"I'm surprised you didn't."

Why hadn't she thought of that? Too late now. She angled her head. "So?"

"Not much to tell."

Brianna shook her head, her mouth curving into a smile. "Really, I've heard that before."

Andrew chuckled. "Yes, you have. Okay, well, I grew up here, in this house, but when I was nineteen, I went travelling. I wanted to see the world."

"Where did you go?"

"Just about everywhere."

"Like Shawn."

"Yes, like Shawn."

"How long did you travel for?"

"Three years."

"Wow. I'm lucky if I get away for two days."

"You should try it sometime. Travel widens your horizons."

"I was going to Spain, remember?"

"That's right, you were." Andrew stopped washing and

looked deep into her eyes, sending her heart-rate flying. "You should go in the spring. It's lovely then."

Brianna's heart thudded as the thought of going with him flitted through her mind. She bit her lip. How could she be even thinking that? She barely knew him, but a longing she'd never felt before took hold within her. *To be close to a man.* It had always frightened her, but she'd never met anyone like Andrew McKinnon. Could God help her to open her heart after all this time? She fought to regain her composure. "I might just do that." She held his gaze, unable to tear away, her heart pounding with a warmth she'd never felt before.

"Hey you two. Have you finished?"

Brianna's eyes widened and she felt her face flush. Grace had caught them staring at each other. She immediately faced the sink and continued wiping the dish in her hand, trying to steady her heart-rate. "Almost." Her voice came out high and shaky.

"Well, we're done. We'll leave you to it."

Brianna glanced over her shoulder. Grace's grin caused her cheeks to flush a second time. "Okay..."

Once Grace and Ryan left, Brianna and Andrew glanced at each other and burst into laughter. His eyes twinkled, and for a long moment they looked at each other and smiled in earnest. "Come on, let's finish up and find a cosy corner to chat."

Was this really happening, or was she dreaming?

CHAPTER 6

*a*ndrew chose a corner in the drawing room near the fire, and he and Brianna talked for hours, drinking copious amounts of hot chocolate while Christmas carols played in the background and the others chatted and played games. The more she learned of him, the more she was drawn to him. She surprised herself and told him about her rape and the baby she lost, her years of drug addiction, and then how his mother, Rosemary, had led her to the Lord, right here, in the Elim Community.

In his soft Scottish brogue, Andrew told her about the years he'd spent away from the Lord, and how close he'd come to getting drawn into the world of drugs and alcohol, but something had stopped him—he believed it was God and the prayers of his parents.

He told her about the walk he did in Spain, where he met God for real. Brianna decided she'd like to do it herself. It sounded awesome, hiking through small villages and across huge mountains. But not alone—*with him.* Andrew exuded all the qualities she could ever want in a man but had never expected to find. Soft-spoken, kind and gentle, and so good-looking. And his job... chef in one of the fanciest restaurants in Glasgow! Not a restaurant she'd ever been to, but she'd heard about it. It was the place people went to for special occasions, where the meals were amazing. But above everything, *he loved God.* And it seemed he liked her... a lot, which made her heart sing. But was it right? Was she racing ahead? Was it what God wanted for her? And there was also the feeling that he was keeping something from her.

As Brianna lay in bed later that night, her heart danced with excitement and anticipation, sleep eluding her as images of Andrew McKinnon played through her mind. But when sleep finally came, her soul was filled with peace. If this was meant to be, she had no doubt that God would lead and guide her.

The following morning, Brianna woke with a start. Someone was staring at her, touching her... Her eyes snapped open, her heart racing, and then she laughed. "Quinn, what are you doing?"

"Mummy won't wake up." His voice was so little, and his dark eyes were round and anxious.

Brianna shivered as she sat. The first hint of daylight peeked through the gap in the curtains. Slipping her gown over her shoulders, she glanced at the clock on her nightstand. Seven a.m. Nothing to worry about, but Quinn obviously was concerned.

"Come and sit up here with me, Quinny. Mummy's just asleep, that's all." Brianna hoped that was all—surely Alana hadn't taken anything? Her brows pinched together. *But what if she had?* She should have spent the evening with her sister, not with Andrew. What had she been thinking? But the thought of Andrew's soft voice and caring eyes sent her heart spinning afresh.

Quinn climbed onto the bed, snuggling close.

Brianna put her arm around the little boy, smoothing his messed-up hair and placing a kiss on top, surprising herself at how natural it felt. "Does Mummy often sleep in?"

Quinn nodded.

"What do you normally do when you wake up?"

"I look at her until she opens her eyes."

Brianna's heart melted. She hated to think how long he stood there.

"Mummy must get tired. I'm sure she'll wake up soon."

"Can you read me a story?" Lifting his head, Quinn looked at her with anticipation.

"Sure. Have you got a book?"

"Yes, I'll go get it." Slipping out from under her arm and onto the floor, he ran around the divider into the partitioned off area he shared with his mum. While he looked, Brianna also poked her head around the divider to allay any fears about Alana. From what she saw, Alana was just asleep. Moments later, Quinn stood up with several books in his hand, and they both returned to Brianna's bed.

"Which one would you like me to read?"

He looked at each of them in turn, and then held up a well-worn copy of *The Poky Little Puppy.*

Memories of Mam reading this very same book to her and Grace when they were little flashed through Brianna's mind. *Surely it's not the actual book?* She quickly flicked it open to the inside front cover and her jaw dropped. Her name, scrawled in messy hand-writing, confirmed it was. Tears welled in her eyes as she lifted a finger and ran it over the scrawl. It seemed like just yesterday she was snuggling close to Mam. She could hear Mam's soft, gentle voice reading the story, feel Mam's arm around her... it wasn't fair that she'd died so young. Brianna sucked in a breath and brushed at her eyes.

Alana and Aislin had been even younger than she and Grace when they all got separated. They probably didn't even remember Mam. What had it been like for them to be sent away at such a young age? Brianna shuddered as she recalled the years she and Grace spent at Aunt Hilda's and prayed that Aislin and Alana had fared better, but somehow, doubted it.

Renewed compassion grew in her heart for her younger sisters, Alana in particular. Only God had saved Brianna from the self-destructive path she'd taken, and only God could heal the deep-seated hurts Alana carried. More prayer was needed.

"Auntie, are you going to read?" Quinn looked up again as he pulled on Brianna's arm, bringing her back to the present.

She hugged him. "Sorry, Quinny. Let's start." Locating page one, she began reading the words she knew so well.

"Five little puppies dug a hole under the fence and went for a walk in the wide, wide world. Through the meadow they went, down the road, over the bridge, across the green grass, and up the hill, one after the other..."

Immersed in the story, Brianna didn't notice Alana leaning

against the wall until Quinn held his arms out and asked her to join them.

Smiling, Brianna patted the empty space on the bed. "Come on, Alana, come and join us."

Alana hesitated for a moment, but then walked to the bed and perched on the edge.

Quinn scrambled up and threw his arms around her neck.

"Quinny, be careful or you'll knock Mummy off the bed."

Alana gave a small chuckle as she hugged him. "He's okay. I love my morning cuddles." She rested her head against his and smiled at Brianna. "Thanks for reading to him." Her voice was soft but hoarse.

"You're welcome. I'm glad you had a lie in."

Alana nodded. "I don't get much of a break now that Aislin's married."

"You must miss her."

Alana nibbled her lower lip. "Yes. We've never been apart until now."

"Much like Grace and me." Brianna rubbed Alana's arm, the sadness in Alana's eyes tugging at her heart. "You'll have to tell me what it was like growing up, but later." She nodded her head towards Quinn.

Alana sniffed and gave Brianna a small, grateful smile.

"I can hear noises downstairs. We'd best go down."

Alana blew her nose and nodded before lifted Quinn's head off her chest. She gently brushed the hair off his forehead and looked into his eyes. "Ready for breakfast, Quinny?"

"Can we finish the book first?" He looked at her with pleading eyes.

She hugged him to her chest, rocking him like a baby. "Later. Okay?"

"Okay." His voice was so sweet, so innocent.

Alana stood and placed Quinn on the floor. Taking his hand, she turned and gave Brianna a nod. "We'll be ready in a few minutes."

Brianna gave her a warm smile. "No hurry."

BRIANNA SAT on her bed and bowed her head, her heart heavy with compassion for Alana. She knew what it was like to be lonely, and she prayed her sister might find peace and love, just like she had when she met Jesus. Rising from her bed, she slipped on a soft-pink cashmere sweater and her favourite pair of jeans, brushed her hair, and applied a little blusher and lipstick. Her mind drifted to Andrew as she dressed and her heart skittered, but then she grew guilty for thinking about him after seeing how deeply lonely Alana was. But only God could truly fill the empty vacuum in a person's heart. The prospect of being loved by someone special was exciting, but faded in comparison to being loved by God. She prayed Alana might come to know that truth for herself.

Shortly after, Brianna, Alana and Quinn headed downstairs for breakfast, each woman taking one of Quinn's hands as they descended the steps. He wanted to be swung, but Alana told him it would be too dangerous, so he just walked down between them. By the time they arrived, just about everybody else was seated at the long table eating breakfast and chatting.

Caitlin looked up from her position near the door and waved them forward, her face jolly as always. "Come in, come in. There's coffee and tea on the sideboard, as well as cereal and toast. Fresh eggs are coming in a moment."

"I'm happy with tea and toast, thanks." Brianna smiled as she headed for the sideboard, but her gaze darted around the table until it connected briefly with Andrew's. She gave him a small nod before turning her attention to the toast and tea, but she couldn't help the tingle of excitement rippling through her.

She poured tea for herself and for Alana, and then popped a piece of pre-cooked toast onto a plate before heading for the vacant seat beside Andrew, surprising herself with her forwardness.

"Good morning. Sleep well?" His soft burr and warm eyes made her heart skitter afresh.

"Yes, and you?"

His eyes twinkled. "Och aye, I fell asleep with a sweet lassie on my mind."

Brianna giggled. The only other person who'd ever called her 'lassie' was Andrew's mother, and she loved the way it rolled off his tongue.

As she sipped her tea, Danny stood, rubbing his hands briskly together. "Good morning, everyone. Hope you all slept well."

Generally favourable responses moved around the table.

"Great to hear. I've got two pieces of good news for you. The first one is that Fraser McAdams is stable in Glasgow Hospital, and his wife gave birth to a healthy baby boy last night. She's been transferred to Glasgow Hospital to be near him."

Audible relief shifted from person to person.

"And here's some other good news... snow fell on the

mountains last night, so skiing will definitely be on the agenda for today."

Once again, everyone reacted positively, apart from Brendan. He leaned back in his chair, folded his arms, and stared at Daniel. "I'd rather go to the pub." Silence fell around the table as all eyes turned to him. It was almost like he was laying down a challenge.

Daniel didn't react. Instead, he just shrugged. "Suit yourself, but we'd like you to come." He sipped his coffee, making a slurping noise, then wrapped his hands around his mug as he glanced out the window. "Should be a good day, although the weather can change at any time. I suggest we head off as soon as we can and make the most of the day, given how short it is this time of year. There's gear in the storeroom for anyone who wants to try their hand at skiing. Otherwise, just grab some thick jackets. If the wind picks up, it can get freezing up there."

"Sounds great, Danny," Grace said, shooting a severe look at Brendan as she pushed her chair back. If anyone could take him on, it would be Grace. "Brendan should be on dishes if he's not coming."

He sighed. "I'll come. I was just stirring."

"Good. But you can still do the dishes." Grace's tone of voice left no room for argument.

"I'll help," Shawn said as he began gathering the dirty plates.

Brianna watched everyone interact as she finished her tea. Not much had changed since they were all children, sparring in the kitchen together at meal times. Grace had always been the boss, and she still was. A tinge of sadness washed over her as she thought about all those lost years. But they were together now, and somehow, they'd all survived. Now she was beginning to feel glad she hadn't gone to Spain after all. She did know them... they were her siblings, her family.

Within half an hour, everyone was ready to leave. Andrew was waiting by the bus for Brianna when she arrived from upstairs with Alana and Quinn. It amazed her how every time his gaze met hers, her heart turned over in response. She gave him a smile and joined him as they climbed into the bus. Despite the cold, she felt wrapped in an invisible warmth as she sat beside him for the short journey to Aonach Mor.

CHAPTER 7

As Brianna sat in the bus with Andrew beside her, Ben Nevis had never looked so majestic. Covered in snow, the bare slopes of the huge mountain dominated the horizon, but it was Aonach Mor, just two peaks from Ben Nevis, they were headed for. In the seat in front, Quinn jiggled on Alana's lap and peeked over her shoulder, smiling coyly at Brianna. When she returned his smile and reached out, tapping the tip of his nose, he giggled and her heart warmed.

Daniel brought the bus to a stop in the parking area already filled with tourist coaches and motorhomes. Everyone stood and began filing out. Brianna's heart missed a beat when Andrew placed his hand briefly on the small of her back as she slipped past him.

Although she wore her thick winter jacket, she shivered when a blast of bitter wind buffeted her as she stepped out of the bus. The Cairngorm range, with snowy peaks towering all around, was much colder than Glasgow.

She smiled when Dillon ran up to Andrew, taking his hand and chatting excitedly as they approached the ticket booth. Andrew didn't seem to mind—in fact, by the way he chatted back, he seemed to enjoy the interaction.

With the tickets bought, they all joined the line of people waiting to catch a gondola up the mountain to the ski fields and restaurant. Daniel allowed everyone to go ahead of him and stood with Andrew and Dillon at the rear. Aislin, Joel, Grace, Ryan, Brendan and Shawn hopped into the first gondola. Caleb, Caitlin and their two girls climbed into the second one. Lizzy, James, Clare, and Lizzy's parents were next in line, leaving Daniel, Andrew, Dillon, Alana, Quinn, and Brianna in the last one.

Daniel motioned for her, Alana, and Quinn to enter first. Brianna followed them in and sat beside Alana. Andrew climbed in and sat directly opposite. Their eyes briefly met, and as they shared a smile, her pulse skittered alarmingly. She'd never seen a man look so good in a hand-knitted beanie and matching scarf. As the gondola jerked and began its journey upwards, she swivelled in her seat to look at the magnificent view, but every now and then her gaze found Andrew's, and each time, a quiver surged through her.

The ride only took fifteen minutes. When the gondola reached the top station and they all began to exit, Brianna tripped and almost lost her footing. Strong hands on her arms steadied her. She turned around to offer her thanks, but as she looked into Andrew's eyes, her voice caught and all she could do was offer a coy grin.

∼

ANDREW STRUGGLED to tear his gaze away from Brianna and listen to Dillon after they exited the gondola. Her shyness and innocence mesmerised him, but Dillon tugged on his sleeve, pulling his attention away. He looked down at the little boy as Brianna walked ahead and joined Grace and Ryan.

"Can you take me skiing, Andrew?" Dillon grabbed his hand and dragged him to the fence where skiers were lining up for the chair lift.

"We'll have to talk to your dad about that. Have you skied before?"

Dillon nodded enthusiastically. "Dad took me last year."

Andrew grinned. "I bet you were good."

"I fell over three times, but I didn't get hurt. Can you take me, please?" He jumped up and down on the spot.

Andrew ruffled Dillon's hair and chuckled. "If you dad says yes, I'll be happy to."

Dillon whooped. "I'll go ask him."

As the boy dashed off to find Daniel, Andrew headed back to the group, his gaze searching for Brianna. When he found her, for a long moment he studied her, drinking in her rosy cheeks and full lips as she crouched in the snow, busily making a snowman with Quinn while everyone else stood around discussing their options. He'd never seen anything so beautiful.

Dillon waved Andrew over to where he was trying to get Daniel's attention. Andrew was torn. He wanted to join Brianna, but didn't want to let Dillon down. He shouldn't have promised. Blowing out a breath, he joined him and Daniel.

Daniel looked up as Andrew approached. "So, I believe Dillon's asked you to take him skiing." Daniel patted the little boy's shoulder. "Don't worry, I'll take him. I'm sure you don't want to be stuck on the beginner slopes."

"I don't mind, really." But that wasn't true... he'd rather build a snowman. He could go skiing anytime he wanted.

Daniel shrugged. "I wouldn't mind going on the red run with the others, so maybe we can take it in turns?"

Andrew bit his lip. "Sure. You go now, I'll go later."

"Thanks. Just keep an eye on him. He thinks he's better than he is." He winked at Dillon and clapped Andrew on the back before moving off to the chairlift with Grace, Ryan, Caleb and Shawn.

A few members of the group left for the beginner slopes, while others headed to the restaurant for hot chocolate and shortbread. Lizzy had joined Brianna and Quinn in the snow, as had James, Clare and Alana. Lizzy motioned for Dillon to join them. "Come on, Dillon, we're making snowmen. Come and join us so Andrew can go skiing."

Brianna looked up with a puzzled but pleased expression. She'd obviously expected him to go skiing with the others.

"It's okay, I'm happy to take him." Andrew placed his hand on Dillon's shoulder, and after shooting Brianna a quick glance, he bent down and looked Dillon in the eye. "How about we make a snowman first, buddy?"

"Yeah, come on Dillon. Come and help us," James called out as he patted a lump of snow onto the snowman's body.

Dillon glanced at the ski field and then at the snowman. "Okay." He threw his skis down and scooped up a big handful of snow, slapping it onto the snowman James was making with Lizzy and Clare.

Andrew put his skis down and hesitated. Dillon seemed to

have forgotten about him, and there were four in that group with Lizzy and only three in Brianna's. It was a no-brainer. He crouched down and joined Brianna.

～

BRIANNA ALMOST HADN'T dared hope that Andrew would join her, so when a shadow fell across the snowman she was building with Alana and Quinn, she took a quick, sharp breath.

He knelt beside her and winked. "Like some help?"

A giddy sense of excitement rushed through her.

Quinn nodded eagerly, saving her from answering. "You can build his arms."

"We'll have to find some sticks for that," Andrew said. "Do you want to come look for some with me?"

"Okay." The little boy stood and took Andrew's hand, angling his head to peer up at the tall man. "Where will we find them?"

"I'm not sure. We might have to look really hard... there aren't many trees around."

"Why aren't there?" Quinn's eyes narrowed and his forehead scrunched.

"That's a long story," Andrew answered as they walked off together.

The way Andrew took all of Quinn's questions in stride warmed Brianna's heart. All the kids loved him, and he seemed to love them. She recalled reading somewhere that you could tell a person's character by the way they treated children and animals. If this was anything to go by, Andrew McKinnon was a good man.

"He's nice," Alana said quietly, as she patted more snow on the snowman's body.

Brianna blinked. Had Alana read her thoughts? "He is."

"He likes you."

Heat raced up Brianna's neck and into her face. "What makes you say that?"

"The way he looks at you."

Brianna shrugged as she balled more snow, all the while keeping her gaze averted. "I hadn't noticed."

Alana chuckled. "Come on, Brianna. Of course you have."

She looked up, unable to hide the grin on her face. "You're right." Maybe she shouldn't be saying this to Alana—it might just make her loneliness more obvious, but then, maybe being honest and sharing would help seal their relationship. "I think I like him too."

Alana focused on the snowman before meeting Brianna's gaze. When she did, her eyes were filled with longing and regret. "I'm happy for you."

"Thanks, but nothing's happened yet."

"It will, I can tell."

"You miss Conall, don't you?"

Alana nodded, wiping a tear from her eye.

Brianna gave her wrist a gentle squeeze. "I'm sure there's someone better out there for you. He doesn't deserve you after what he did." Brianna would have preferred to tell Alana that Jesus loved her, but it was too premature—they barely knew each other, and somehow it didn't seem like the right time. *But when was the right time?* She prayed God would let her know.

She glanced at Andrew chatting easily with Quinn while

the two of them looked for sticks. A tinge of guilt flowed through her. She quickly put it aside.

When Andrew and Quinn returned moments later with some small twigs, Brianna couldn't deny the spark of excitement rising in her.

The next half hour or so passed happily. Brianna laughed and joked with everyone, including Andrew. When it came time for judging whose snowman was the best, they all agreed they were both great in their own way and both were winners.

Lizzy stood and brushed snow off her jacket and pants. "It must be time for a hot drink. It's freezing out here." She rubbed her hands together briskly.

"Can't we go skiing, Mum? Andrew was going to take me." Dillon pleaded with her.

"After we've had something to eat and drink, Dillon. Okay?" Lizzy gave him a stern look.

Dillon hung his head. "Okay."

They gathered their belongings and tramped through the snow up to the restaurant. After placing the skis in the racks, they headed inside into the warmth of the restaurant, joining Lizzy's parents, and Caitlin and Brendan, at a table near a large picture window with a panoramic view of the ski fields.

Dillon headed straight for the window and stared out at the skiers weaving down the mountain. James, Clare and Quinn joined him.

When Andrew pulled a chair out for her, Brianna's mouth curved into a smile before she lowered her gaze. It was nice having a handsome Scotsman look after her.

The adults ordered coffees, and the children, hot chocolates. Scones with clotted cream and strawberry jam were ordered all round. They'd just finished eating when the skiers returned.

"How was it?" Andrew asked, when they all traipsed in and pulled up chairs to join the group.

"Great," Danny replied, shrugging off his jacket before he sat. "How was the boy?" He nodded towards Dillon.

"We just built snowmen." Dillon leaned on Daniel, his bottom lip protruding in a pout.

Daniel picked him up and plopped him on his lap. "That must have been fun."

"Not as much fun as skiing."

"It was my fault. I wanted to make a snowman," Andrew confessed.

Daniel held in a chuckle.

Brianna picked at her nails to avoid looking at him. Danny would easily figure out why Andrew chose to make a snowman over skiing. She hoped he wouldn't joke about it in front of everyone.

A child screamed at the next table and everyone turned to see what had happened. A toddler had fallen off his chair and landed heavily on the floor. By the time he stopped crying, the previous conversation had been forgotten, and Brianna relaxed when everyone started chatting amongst themselves.

A little later, when Andrew leaned close and whispered in her ear inviting her to ski one of the runs with him, she agreed without a second thought.

CHAPTER 8

*A*fter Brianna quickly organised a set of skis, she and Andrew hurried to the chairlift where Grace, Ryan, Caleb, Shawn, Joel and Aislin stood in a group chatting.

Ryan looked up as they approached. "About time! We were just about to go without you."

"Sorry we held you up," Andrew said, his voice low and humourless.

Grace nudged Ryan in the ribs. "We weren't about to go. Ryan was just trying to be funny."

He clapped Andrew on the back and chuckled. "Like Grace said, I was just being silly. It's all good. Thought we'd do the blue run this time. Sound all right?"

"Is it an easy one?" Brianna asked.

"You worried, Bi?"

Straightening, she lifted her chin. "No..." But if it hadn't been for Andrew inviting her, she most definitely would not be standing there about to ski down a mountain, no matter how easy the run might be.

"Okay, let's go." Ryan led the way and they all skied to the line. Within a matter of minutes, Brianna was sitting beside Andrew, being swept upwards over the dazzling white snow, skis swinging in the air below the seat.

"Are you okay?" He turned his head and searched her eyes.

She felt a ripple of excitement. Was Andrew about to hold her hand? Kiss her? How romantic would that be? How had this happened? White snowy peaks, brilliant against the pale blue sky, fresh mountain air brushing her face and heightening her senses, a gorgeous, caring man seated beside her, gazing into her eyes... *Was she okay?* She was more than okay. She surprised herself and smiled easily. "Yes, but I have to confess I'm not good at skiing."

"That's okay. I've done a bit of skiing. I can help."

Brianna let out a happy sigh. Warmth flooded her body, and she pulled her gaze away to look at the scenery. Minutes later they disembarked and joined the others, but as she stood beside them, a lump grew in the pit of her stomach as the reality of what she'd committed herself to hit home. *Why had she thought she could do this?*

Grace adjusted her goggles, nodded to Ryan, and together they took off down the mountain, looking like pros. Caleb and Shawn went next, followed by Joel and Aislin. When just the two of them were left, Andrew looked at Brianna and tilted his head. "Ready?"

She steeled herself but her insides quivered. "I... I guess so." She lowered her goggles and eased forward. Her heart pounded. The hill was so steep. *Why was she doing this?* As her speed increased, she tried to remember how to snow plough, but she panicked and angled her skis to the side, coming to an abrupt stop and landing headfirst in the snow.

Lifting her head, she brushed snow off her face as tears pricked her eyes. She shouldn't have come.

Andrew stopped beside her and bent down, his face etched with worry. "What happened, Brianna? Are you hurt?"

"No, but I shouldn't have come. I'm sorry." She tried to sit, but her skis were so long and she couldn't get them into the right position. She flopped back into the snow, close to tears.

Andrew reached out his hand. "Let me help you up. I didn't realise you couldn't ski at all. But it's okay, I can show you."

Brianna shook her head. "No... I'll climb back to the top and go down on the chair lift."

"They won't let you. Here, take my hand—I'll help you." His voice was so kind and sincere, and he didn't sound annoyed.

She took his hand. Finally getting her skis facing the right direction, she slipped when she tried to stand and collapsed back onto the snow. This time, instead of crying, she laughed as her skis went in opposite directions. "I'm sorry. I really am useless."

Andrew laughed with her. "No, you're not. Use your poles and I'll steady you. Bend your knees and keep your weight low. It's all about your centre of gravity."

"Okay... I'll try again." She sat, then slowly eased herself up with Andrew's help until she was upright and stable. "Thank you."

"My pleasure." He grinned at her. "Now, tell me what you know."

"Not much, I'm afraid."

"Okay, we'll take it really slowly. We'll need to keep out of the way of the faster skiers, but it'll be fine. We'll just do short runs, and we can take a break whenever you want."

"I'm so sorry."

Andrew gave her a smile that made her knees even weaker, if that was possible. "I don't mind. We can take as long as you need. Ready?"

She nodded.

"Okay, we'll just go a few metres, then we'll stop, turn, and go another few metres until you get the hang of it. I'll go first and I can help you stop if needed." He lowered his goggles and effortlessly skied a short distance before stopping and turning, and waited for her to reach him.

Brianna inched forward, trying to keep the skis angled in a little as she steadied herself with her poles. Going sideways was much less frightening than going straight down. As she approached Andrew, she slowed and then stopped.

"How was that?"

She smiled. "Better."

"Good. Now we need to change directions. It's easier to do when you're moving, so we'll keep going in this direction, then when you're ready, turn your left ski first, bend your leg, then bring your right ski around until they're parallel again. We won't go fast, so it'll be okay. I'll go first."

Andrew made it look so easy. Brianna squared her shoulders and steeled herself. Surely she could do it. She inhaled slowly then eased forward. Her heart ricocheted in her chest as she began turning her left ski. What if she couldn't bring it around and she ended up going straight down? She could kill herself. *No... don't think like that...*

concentrate. Bend your knees. Bring the skis around. The tension in her body eased a little when she was facing the opposite direction.

Andrew rested one arm on his pole and gave her a high five as she pulled up next to him.

"I did it." Her gentle laugh rippled through the air.

"You did." His eyes sparkled and her heart skipped a beat. "Ready to do another one?"

"Yes," she replied, feeling a lot more confident.

"Let's go."

She followed him down a slightly longer run, but her ski got stuck and she tumbled, landing at his feet, face first in the snow once again. She lifted her head slowly, wiping snow off her face.

Andrew bent down and helped her sit. "Are you okay? Nothing broken?"

Brianna felt her ankle. It was a little tender, but not broken. "I'm fine. Just embarrassed."

"It was a very elegant fall."

"No, it wasn't! How can a face-plant be elegant?" She broke into an involuntary giggle.

"Depends on who's doing it." His eyes sparkled with merriment.

Brianna's breath caught as their eyes met. The magnetism between them was growing, and it scared and excited her at the same time. "You're... you're such a good skier. Where did you learn?"

"Italy, mainly. It's great over there. Bigger ski fields than here. Lots of runs." He reached out and flicked some snow off her hair. "You should check it out."

Brianna giggled. "Bigger runs wouldn't be any good for me, but I'd love to go to Italy. It must be lovely."

"It would be even lovelier when sharing it with someone special."

Her heart beat faster. Was he just flirting, or was he for real? He'd have the pick of any number of girls in his line of work. Maybe he wasn't serious at all and he was just amusing himself with her. Filling in time. He seemed genuine, but really, what did she know about him? *Zilch.*

She jumped when a spray of snow hit her in the face. Grace and Ryan pulled up in front of them, looking anxious. "Bibi, we've been looking everywhere for you."

Brianna angled her head. "Why? What's wrong?"

"A storm's coming—didn't you notice?" Grace's annoyed glance darted between her and Andrew.

"No." But a quick look at the sky confirmed Grace was right. A thick band of cloud hovered threateningly over Ben Nevis and was heading their way. How had they missed it? "Thanks for letting us know. I got stuck, and Andrew's been helping me. We'll follow you down."

"Good. Don't waste any time. We're off to find Aislin and Joel and we'll be right down."

"We won't—we'll come straight away." Brianna grabbed her poles.

"See you there." Grace lifted her hand in a wave and propelled herself forward. Ryan followed, and within moments, they were out of sight.

Brianna looked at Andrew. "How did we miss those angry-looking clouds?" But she knew... they'd been so distracted with each other they hadn't noticed it.

Andrew shrugged and looked apologetic. "I should have paid more attention. We'd better get moving." He sounded worried. Quickly standing, he offered her his gloved hand.

Brianna took it and tried hard not to get her skis tangled as he helped her up. "I hope we make it back in time. The sky looks menacing." Her chest tightened.

"We'll be okay, but we'll need to go faster." A muscle in his jaw quivered.

"I'll do my best." Taking some deep breaths, she tried to avoid looking too far down the hill.

"You'll be fine. I'll be beside you the whole way."

"Thanks." Brianna gave him a nervous smile and eased carefully forward. As her confidence grew, she took longer, steeper runs before changing direction, but was still unable to go straight down like the other skiers. Before reaching the half-way mark, wind gusts carrying icy bullets of snow and ice pummelled them, reducing visibility and sending the temperature plummeting. When the lights from the restaurant pierced the cloud, she released a huge sigh of relief. She thought she was never going to make it.

Daniel waved frantically as they approached the gondola station, motioning them to hurry. "Quick, the last gondola's about to leave." His voice barely reached them.

Brianna dipped her chin against the wind and skied the short distance to join him. He gave her shoulder a squeeze and then peered behind her, his forehead puckering. "Where are Grace and Ryan?"

Brianna's forehead creased. "They went looking for Aislin and Joel."

"Aislin and Joel are fine—they caught the last gondola with

the others, but Grace and Ryan aren't here." Daniel's voice was thick with emotion. He peered up the mountain as the gondola operator ushered them onto the landing. Turning around, he pushed against the man. "There's two more to come... we have to wait." Brianna had never seen Daniel so agitated.

The short, chubby man shook his head. "We can't wait, sorry. This is the last one going down. I'll report them as missing and send a team out. Just give me the details."

Brianna's eyes popped open. *Missing? Grace and Ryan?* The gondola lurched when she stepped into it, and without thinking, she grabbed Andrew's arm.

Daniel held his ground. "I want to stay. I'm sure they'll be here any minute." His usual kind voice was surprisingly curt.

But even his charm didn't work on the man. "Like I said, I'll report them as missing. The Mountain Rescue Team will go looking for them and will bring them down. Where were they last seen?" He ushered Daniel into the gondola as he spoke.

Daniel looked to Andrew.

Andrew took the cue. "They were about three hundred metres from the start of the blue run when we saw them. They're good skiers, so I don't know what would have happened."

"We'll find them, don't you worry." After the man closed the gate and pressed a button, the gondola lurched forward.

Daniel ran his hand over his thick woollen beanie as they began to descend, his eyes wide and glassy. "I don't believe this has happened."

Tears pricked Brianna's eyes. It was all her fault. What if something happened to them? She'd never forgive herself. She brushed her tears away quickly, but too late, because Andrew had noticed. He took her hand and squeezed it. "They'll be okay. Ryan seems resourceful and he knows these mountains, and your sister's strong. They'll be fine."

She nodded, wanting to believe him, but she couldn't help but fear the worst as the wind gusts increased and visibility reduced to zero.

CHAPTER 9

With the wind buffeting the gondola, the ride down Aonach Mor was scarier than the rides at Alton Towers. Daniel, Brianna and Andrew held hands and prayed not only for their safety, but that of Grace and Ryan's. Brianna could barely utter a word, but her heart pleaded with God to keep them safe. If only she hadn't gone up there in the first place. What had she been thinking? She owed her life to Grace. A heavy weight settled in her stomach. How many times had Grace dragged her out of the gutter after she'd overdosed following the loss of her baby? Sat beside her in hospital when she should have been at work? Cared enough to bring her to Danny and Lizzy's when neither of them believed in God's power, but it was the only option left? Brianna squeezed her eyes shut and fought back tears. Surely God wouldn't let anything happen to Grace now after all they'd been through?

As they approached the bottom of the mountain, she

inhaled deeply and tried to leave her worry with God. Bible verses she'd committed to memory challenged her to trust Him, but could she? Trusting God in small things was one matter, but now her sister's life was in danger. That was a different story. She had no doubt God worked in people's lives —He'd worked in hers, but would He answer their prayers and keep Grace and Ryan safe in this blizzard? Did he really answer prayers like that?

The gondola came to a stop, and Daniel and Andrew both motioned for her to alight first. Snow swirled on a freezing wind, virtually blowing her off the step. When Andrew grabbed her arm and steadied her, Brianna looked up and gave him a weak, but grateful smile.

Joel, Aislin, Shawn and Caleb stood huddled together and looked up expectantly as the three of them approached. The questions in their eyes quickly changed to alarm as Danny conveyed the news that Grace and Ryan were still on the mountain.

"We need to report them as missing," Caleb said, his eyes large and wild. "It's supposed to get worse."

"The report's been made, but I don't know what's happening. We need to find out." Daniel rubbed his arms briskly as his glance shot to the Aonach Mor Ticket office, now shrouded in heavy cloud.

"I'll come with you." Caleb turned to the others. "Get in the bus and go home. We'll wait here until they're found."

Brianna shook her head. "I want to wait too."

Caleb placed his hand on her shoulder. "No, Bi. You're better off at home, out of this. It could be hours."

"Caleb's right, Bi. We'll let you know as soon as they're found. Go home and pray." Danny's voice was firm, and even though she would rather have stayed, Brianna allowed Andrew to guide her to the bus, the only vehicle remaining in the car park.

A hush fell amongst those waiting inside the bus as the five of them entered. It must have been clear from their faces that something was amiss.

When Andrew cleared his voice, everyone turned their attention to him, Brianna included. With Danny, Caleb and Ryan absent, Andrew took charge, and despite the situation, her insides glowed with pride.

He gave the group a reassuring smile. "I don't want any of you to worry, but Grace and Ryan didn't make the last gondola."

Stunned silence filled the bus.

"Will they be okay?" Dillon's little voice came from one of the front seats.

Andrew looked down at him. "The Mountain Rescue Team will find them." He spoke with quiet confidence.

"Will they come down by helicopter?"

"Maybe."

"Where's my daddy?"

"He and your Uncle Caleb are waiting here until they come down the mountain. He said for the rest of us to go home and get warm and dry."

"Can I stay with them?" Dillon's little voice inched higher.

"Dillon!" Lizzy glared at him. "That's enough. We're going home like Daddy said."

"Okay." Dillon's shoulders slumped.

Andrew rubbed his hands together. "We'll need to get the chains on the tyres—it's going to be a hairy ride home. Everyone understand?" His gaze travelled around the bus. There was a general nod of consensus. Maybe it was because he was Scottish and this was his home, but it seemed that everyone, not just Brianna, was relieved that he was taking charge.

"I'll help." Brendan stood and headed for the front. Brianna was surprised he could walk straight given the number of drinks he'd had, but then, this was Brendan.

"Wait for me." Shawn stood and joined him.

Andrew nodded in appreciation. "We won't be long."

After the three men exited the bus, those remaining talked in hushed tones. Brianna learned that Lizzy's parents had left early, taking James and Clare with them. Concern grew when Aislin and Joel stated they hadn't seen Grace and Ryan on the mountain. Brianna's chest grew heavy once more until she remembered God was looking after them.

GRACE MOANED as she lay flat on her back in the snow, wincing as pain shot through her right shoulder when she tried to move. Snow swirled all around, and she could barely see a foot above her. Tiny darts of ice, like needles, pelted her in the face. Her chest tightened as panic set in. *Ryan... where's Ryan?* She called out, but the howling gale stole her voice. She placed her hands over her stomach and bit back tears. Cold seeped into her body and she shivered uncontrollably. How had this happened? One minute they'd been skiing down the hill looking for Aislin and Joel, and the next, a mighty gust of wind blew her off-track and sent her flying... now she had no idea where she was, nor where Ryan was, and she couldn't move.

Ryan had to be all right. After everything she'd been through... the horrid years at Aunt Hilda's, Brianna's rape, the bomb... and then finding God, and Ryan. No, she couldn't lose him now, *especially now*... Trying to pull herself up again, she cried out as pain shot across her shoulders and down her arm. No, she couldn't move. Ryan would have to find her. She whimpered. *God, please help him find me...*

Sometime later, Grace thought she heard a voice calling her name. A glimmer of hope washed through her but quickly faded. She must have been hallucinating. But then, moments later, relief flooded her body when Ryan's face loomed over hers.

He cupped her face and planted kisses all over it. "Grace... thank God." The warmth of his breath was like nothing she'd ever known. She stifled a scream as he covered her body with his, transferring his heat to her. Life slowly returned to her bones. She wouldn't die out here after all.

Lifting his head, Ryan stroked her face and gazed lovingly into her eyes. "I looked everywhere for you. One minute you were beside me, next minute you were gone. Are you hurt?"

Grace looked back at him, nodding as best she could. "My... my shoulder..."

"I'm sorry, darling, I'm leaning on you." He eased himself off her. "Which one?"

"Right."

"You can't move?"

She shook her head ever so slightly. Despite Ryan's gentle manner, Grace flinched as he felt the injured area. She didn't need him to confirm she'd broken something. The look on his face when he straightened said it all. But at least they were together.

"Any pain in your back?"

"I don't think so. Just my shoulder and arm." Her lips were so cold she could hardly move them.

"I think you've broken your collarbone."

"Oh…" Her voice was small. "What are we going to do?"

"Get you off the snow for a start. It'll hurt, but I've got to lift you off it or you'll freeze to death. I'll grab some branches and place them under you. Are you okay while I go find some?"

She blinked, and it felt like her eyelashes were frozen. "Don't be long."

Lowering his face, he kissed her gently, warming her lips. "I'll be right back, but before I go, I'll wrap you in this." Taking out a small package from his backpack, Ryan removed a thin, silver piece of plastic which flapped wildly in the gale until he managed to secure it around her.

"I should have known you'd come prepared." Her teeth chattered.

"Once a soldier, always a soldier." Blue eyes she'd come to love so much winked at her. "Better?"

She nodded and gave him a weak smile. "Thank you."

"You're welcome. Now, I'll go and grab those branches. I'll be back in a jiffy."

Although she knew Ryan wouldn't go far, fear of losing sight of him outweighed any pain she might experience by turning her head and keeping him in sight. She bit back pain as she watched him stumble through the fresh snow to reach the pine bushes only metres away. Despite the emergency blanket blocking most of the wind, Grace still shivered uncontrollably. Ryan was right... they could die out here. Visibility was so low no one would find them, and early dark was already setting in.

Breaking off several branches, he carried them back and knelt beside her. "I'm going to put these under you. I'll try not to hurt you, but I can't promise."

Grace nodded and tried to prepare herself for the pain, biting down on her lip to stop screaming as he rolled her gently onto her left side. He slid the branches under her before rolling her back. The relief of being off the freezing snow was worth the pain.

"I'll grab some bigger branches now and make a shelter."

She looked up at him with pride. "You're... quite the boy scout." Her voice wobbled as her teeth continued to click together.

His mouth twisted in a smile. "Survival training, Grace."

"I'm glad you know what to do."

"I'll be back in a minute."

After Ryan returned with some larger branches, he wedged them into the snow and huddled down beside her, careful not to hurt her as he placed an arm across her body, drawing close to her as he gazed into her eyes. "I thought I'd lost you."

Her throat was so cold and sore, she could barely reply. "I thought I'd died."

"Thank God you didn't. I love you, Grace."

"And I love you, Ryan." She swallowed hard. "There's something..." She swallowed again. "There's something I need to tell you..."

"What is it, love? What's the matter?"

"I... I was keeping it as a Christmas present, but you need to know. Just in case..." She sucked in a breath and felt a sharp pain in her chest.

In the rapidly fading light, she could just make out his furrowed brow.

He stroked her cheek. "Tell me love, what is it?"

"I... I hope nothing's happened..." Her lips trembled. "I'm... I'm pregnant."

Ryan's eyes enlarged. "Pregnant?"

Grace nodded, pushing back the tears stinging her eyes. "I hope I haven't lost the baby."

"Oh Grace, I'm sure he or she will be fine. Pregnant? Really?" Intensity radiated from his bright eyes.

"I shouldn't have gone skiing."

"You didn't know this was going to happen." He traced her cheek with his finger before kissing her forehead gently. "That little baby is well protected in there."

"It was supposed to be a surprise."

He gave her a smile that spoke straight to her heart. "It is a surprise. Telling me a day early hasn't spoiled it at all." He stroked her hair. "And you know what?"

Grace shook her head.

"We'll remember this moment forever." Leaning closer, Ryan kissed her softly on the lips before cradling her head against his chest. He began to hum the tune to *Silent Night, Holy Night* as the wind howled around them.

"All is calm, all is bright..." Grace's voice was quiet and weak,

but the words of the carol filled her with peace. Everything would be all right—God was on their side.

Sometime later, Grace didn't know how long, a flicker of light penetrated the darkness and an overwhelming wave of relief washed over her. *Thank you, God. All is calm, all is bright.*

CHAPTER 10

*B*ack at the house, the atmosphere was subdued as the family sat around the kitchen table. Even Brendan, who'd had more than a few drinks up on the mountain, was quieter than normal. Having two of their group missing in a blizzard was the last thing anyone had expected when they'd set off that morning for a day in the snow, and everyone's thoughts and prayers were with Grace and Ryan.

Lizzy forced herself to remain positive. When the phone rang, she raced to answer it, placing her hand over the mouthpiece to let everyone know it was Daniel. But there was no news, other than to let her know that the Lochaber Mountain Rescue Team was out searching for Grace and Ryan. Daniel was annoyed and disappointed that he and Caleb hadn't been allowed to accompany them.

Lizzy turned her back, keeping her voice low. "Did you really expect they'd let you go with them?"

"Yes. We know what we're doing."

Her hands tightened on the receiver. "Let them do their job, Daniel. They're trained to do this." Sometimes her husband was just too sure of himself, even though he meant well.

"It's just annoying, that's all. We could be out there helping." She could imagine him raking his hands through his hair.

"What, and put yourselves at risk?"

Silence. She was pushing the boundaries, casting doubt on Daniel's abilities, but surely, he'd see it was better for him and Caleb to stay safe. They were both fathers, and the Mountain Rescue Team did this type of thing often. Putting themselves at risk needlessly would be foolish and possibly even selfish, although Lizzy was sure they didn't see it that way.

"You're right, Liz. I'm sorry. You know how bad I am at waiting." He sounded apologetic, slightly downcast.

Lizzy let out a relieved sigh. "I know." Daniel would go stir-crazy if they had long to wait. "Hopefully they'll be found quickly."

"That's what we're praying for."

"As are we." Closing her eyes, she sent up another silent prayer. "Keep us posted, Daniel."

"I will."

When she turned around, all eyes were on her. She gave a small shrug and shook her head, biting back the pent-up emotion welling within her. What if Grace and Ryan weren't found quickly? What if they lay injured somewhere and weren't found until it was too late? Lizzy wrung her hands. No, she couldn't allow herself to think like that. They *would* be found. God was with them and was looking after them. She just had to trust. How important, in times like these when faith was tested, to truly practice what she believed. She prayed she wouldn't be found wanting.

Lizzy forced herself to sound positive when Clare asked if Auntie Grace and Uncle Ryan would miss Christmas. "I'm sure they'll be back soon, sweetheart," she answered, lifting Clare onto her lap and pulling her close.

ANDREW'S PARENTS, Rosemary and David, had joined the group in the kitchen while Lizzy was on the phone. Having lived in the area all their lives, they knew the procedures for a search and rescue, and did their best to assure everyone the Mountain Rescue Team knew what they were doing and would find Grace and Ryan as quickly as they could. "However, saying that, we should continue praying. Conditions often change rapidly in the mountains," David said, his thick Scottish brogue doing little to soften the sobering statement.

Caitlin and Gwyneth, who were busily making cups of tea for everyone, stopped and took a seat. Lizzy glanced around the table. No doubt Brendan and Shawn, and possibly the girls and Joel, would feel uncomfortable, but surely with the seriousness of the situation, they'd put their discomfort aside and stay.

They did. "I'll start if you like," Lizzy said. Bowing her head, she took a slow breath. "Dear God, our hearts are filled with worry over Grace and Ryan, out there somewhere in this blizzard." Her voice was soft and she struggled to speak. "You know where they are. Please wrap your arms around them and protect them from danger. Fill them with your peace, and keep them safe." The inside of her mouth felt as dry as sawdust. "Please help the Mountain Rescue Team find them and bring them home in time for Christmas. Lord, give us peace at this special time of the year as we prepare to celebrate the birth of Jesus. May we truly see your power and might at work in this situation. In Jesus' precious name, Amen." She wiped her eyes as a round of subdued *Amens* followed.

Roger cleared his throat and began praying. Even to Lizzy, her father sounded posh. She prayed the others wouldn't care. "Our dear Lord and heavenly Father, we beseech You to bring Grace and Ryan back to us safely. And be with the rescue team. Guide them and lead them to wherever Grace and Ryan might be. And please bless those of us who are waiting for news. Help us to trust You and to keep Grace and Ryan in our prayers and close to our hearts. In Jesus' name, Amen."

Lizzy brushed another tear from her eye before lifting her head. Never in a million years had she expected her well-bred, arrogant father to have his heart softened by the Almighty God, but she should have—because wasn't that what God did? It was the message of Christmas... God reaching out to a fallen world by sending His perfect son, Jesus, to earth, offering all those who believed in Him new hearts and new lives.

David prayed next, followed by Andrew, who was holding Brianna's hand. Tears streamed down her cheeks. From what she'd told Lizzy when they arrived at the house, Lizzy knew she was blaming herself, but she shouldn't. It was no one's fault that Grace and Ryan were missing.

After the prayer time ended, Caitlin and Gwyneth resumed

making tea. Everyone remained at the table chatting quietly, expecting the phone to ring at any minute. It wasn't how Lizzy had planned to spend Christmas Eve. Instead of the roast chicken dinner she and Caitlin had thought they'd be serving, they had toasties and tatties with grilled cheese. Everybody's appetite had fled.

THE PHONE RANG again as the dishes were being cleared after dinner. Lizzy sprang and answered. Her eyes lit up and she nodded. "That's fantastic news." Covering the mouthpiece with her hand, she shared the news that Grace and Ryan had been found. Loud cheers shattered the air. She returned her attention to Daniel on the other end of the phone.

"They think Grace has broken her collarbone," he told her.

"Oh, no. That's terrible. Poor Grace. Has the wind dropped up there?"

"It's dropping, but it's still too risky for the helicopter. They'll bring her down on the snowmobile and rush her to the hospital."

"Well, it's great news they've been found. I guess you and Caleb will stay with her and Ryan?"

"If we're not needed at home."

"The children are missing you, but you need to be there for Grace."

"Yes, we agree."

"A great way to spend Christmas Eve." Lizzy grimaced as she thought about all the fun things they'd planned for the evening.

"Better than stranded on a mountain."

"You have a point," Lizzy conceded.

"I'll keep you posted, Liz. Tell the kids they need to go to bed early so Santa will come."

"Daniel!" Lizzy turned and faced the wall so the others wouldn't hear.

"Only joking."

"Well, don't! Not now..." She let out a frustrated sigh but then followed it with a small chuckle. Did it really matter?

"Sorry, love." He sounded apologetic.

"Apology accepted."

"I need to go. Love you."

"Love you, too." Lizzy hung the phone up and sent up a prayer of thanks.

$$\sim$$

BRIANNA COULDN'T HELP IT. As she listened to Lizzy on the phone, tears spilled down her cheeks. It was the best news ever. *Grace was safe.* She silently thanked God, and apologised for doubting Him. She wasn't the only one with tears. Alana also wiped her eyes, as did Caitlin.

When Lizzy turned around, a broad smile filled her face. "I'm sure you all heard that. Grace and Ryan are safe. Grace has a broken collarbone, but apart from that, they're both okay. She'll be taken to the hospital as soon as the rescue team can get them off the mountain, and hopefully she'll be home for Christmas."

The children whooped, and everyone visibly relaxed. In an instant, the feeling in the room changed from worry to relief.

"We need to thank Jesus," Dillon stood quietly beside Lizzy and locked eyes with her.

"Yes, we do. You're right. Let's do that now." Her gaze travelled quickly around the table before she placed her hands on his shoulders and bowed her head. "Dear Lord, thank you so much that Grace and Ryan have been found, and that they're both all right. Thank you for looking after them and for leading the Rescue Team to them. We're very grateful. In Jesus' name, Amen." Her voice was so much more upbeat than in her earlier prayer.

A round of enthusiastic *Amen's* followed. Brianna was surprised to hear Brendan and Shawn utter the words.

The children were eager to go to the hospital, but Lizzy told them they needed to go to bed early.

"So Santa will come?" Clare asked.

"Can't we go to the hospital and sing Christmas carols to all the sick people?" Dillon asked. "Santa isn't real anyway."

James and Clare looked up, their eyes questioning. A hush fell over the room as everyone waited for Lizzy's response.

"That's a great idea, Dillon, and yes, you're right... Santa isn't real." She reached out and squeezed James' and Clare's hands. "But it's fun to pretend he is."

Clare burst out crying. "Does that mean we won't get any presents?"

"Oh sweetheart. It doesn't mean that at all. You'll still get your presents, and if you want to believe Santa's real, that's okay."

"Why did Dillon say he's not real?" Clare flashed her brother an angry look as she mixed her words with sobs.

"Maybe because of what's happened with Auntie Grace.

Sometimes when serious things happen, we say things we might not normally say."

"Is Auntie Grace going to be all right?"

"She's going to be fine."

She nodded and wiped at her damp cheeks. "I don't mind if Santa isn't real as long as Auntie Grace is here."

Lizzy pulled Clare back onto her lap and hugged her. "She'll be here when you wake up in the morning."

"That's good. Can we go and sing to her?"

Lizzy kissed the top of her head. "It's too late to do that, sweetheart, but we can sing Christmas carols here. We can light our candles and hang our stockings, just like we planned."

"But Daddy isn't here."

"No, but Grandfather is, and Uncle Shawn, and Uncle Brendan, and everybody else. We'll still have tons of fun, and we can light extra candles for Daddy and Uncle Caleb and Auntie Grace and Uncle Ryan."

"Okay."

Brianna brushed at her own eyes. Andrew slipped a warm hand into hers, squeezing gently and rubbing his thumb lightly over her skin. The sensation filled her with warm fuzziness.

She didn't want the moment to end, but as they all gathered in the drawing room and sang Christmas carols, lit candles and hung stockings, Brianna grew more certain she was smitten with Andrew McKinnon. Not only was he handsome, but watching him lead the singing and read to the children made her wonder if there was anything he couldn't do.

CURLED up in a corner of a couch, surrounded by assorted

cushions and lap blankets, her gaze was fixed on Andrew on the floor with Clare perched on his lap, and James, Dillon and Quinn leaning on him as he told them the story of the Three Wise Men seeking Jesus. But she still sensed he was hiding something. She couldn't put her finger on it, but the occasional shadow that crossed his face hinted that something concerned him. He seemed weighed down, although he hid it well.

But she didn't know him, and she didn't want to get hurt. Maybe it was best to forget about him... Brianna's mind whirled with confused thoughts, but when Andrew's eyes lifted and caught hers, her heart lurched afresh and she knew she couldn't. All she wanted was for him to hold her, to kiss her... Her pulse raced.

Brianna looked up as Rosemary sat on the couch next to her and smiled.

Rosemary patted her leg. "I haven't had a chance to talk with you much, Brianna. How are you doing, lassie?" Her soft brogue warmed Brianna's heart as it always had.

Straightening, she blinked and gathered her thoughts. Had Rosemary noticed her attraction to Andrew? Of course, Rosemary would have... but did she approve? "I'm... I'm doing well. Especially now that Grace has been found."

"I could see you were worried."

"It was my fault." Brianna's voice wavered as she shot a quick glance at Andrew.

"Nobody thinks that, lassie. Don't blame yourself." Rosemary also cut a glance at her son on the floor, her mouth twitching with amusement. "I can see you're taken with each other."

Brianna felt the heat rushing to her face. "I... don't know what to say..."

"You don't need to say anything, lassie. Just let it happen. I'm happy about it."

Relief washed through Brianna. She was getting ahead of herself, but if things worked out, Rosemary could become her mother—how wonderful would that be! To have a mother after all these years. And not just any mother, it would be Rosemary! God was indeed good.

When Andrew finished his story, Brianna quickly gathered her thoughts and gave Rosemary a grateful smile. If Andrew could read her mind it could all come undone. She'd need to be more careful, because what if he didn't feel the same way?

Lizzy announced it was bedtime for the children, and they all asked Andrew to put them to bed. Brianna's cheeks flushed again when he invited her to join him. He must feel the same way, but there was little chance of keeping whatever they had private. She stood, taking Quinn's and James' hands, while Andrew held Clare's and Dillon's. Lizzy and Alana followed behind, chatting quietly as they all walked down the hallway towards the bedrooms.

After settling the children, and assuring them that Auntie Grace and Uncle Ryan would be there in the morning to watch them open their presents, Andrew grabbed Brianna's hand. He held her back, letting Lizzy and Alana go on ahead down the hallway. In the subdued lighting, Brianna's heart pounded, her imagination running wild. Was Andrew about to kiss her? Her heart thumped as she looked expectantly into his eyes, a shiver rippling through her body. The breath caught in her throat. The anticipation was almost unbearable.

But instead of kissing her, he asked if she'd like to go to the hospital to be there when Grace arrived. Brianna bit back her disappointment. Of course he wasn't about to kiss her... what was she thinking? She blinked and quietly said, "That would be great."

His eyes were tender and soft. "I know how much you want to see Grace."

A fresh wave of respect for him washed through Brianna as she chastised herself. He wasn't just handsome and great with the children, he was sensitive as well. "Yes, I do."

"Then, let's go. We'll let the others know on our way out."

"Should we ask if anyone would like to come?" If she were honest, she didn't want them to. The thought of spending time alone with Andrew was more than appealing, but asking would be the right thing to do.

His eager expression changed as his eyes searched hers. "I guess we should." He stroked her hand with his thumb. "Come on, let's go."

He kept hold of her hand as they strode to the top of the staircase. Stopping abruptly, he swung her to face him, his hands gripping her upper arms, the expression on his face a mix of eagerness and tenderness.

Brianna's pulse skittered as Andrew lowered his head and pressed his lips against hers, gently covering her mouth. Shocked by her fervent response, she tried for a moment to pull away, but then gave in and returned his kiss, disappointment filling her when he ended it.

Andrew's chest heaved as he gazed into her eyes. "I've been wanting to do that all day. I'm sorry." He sounded breathless.

Brianna's eyes widened. "Don't be sorry. You can do it again if you like." Her boldness surprised her.

His gaze intensified before lowering his mouth hungrily over hers.

Returning his kiss with reckless abandon, Brianna was transported on a soft, wispy cloud to another world she never knew existed.

When Andrew released her, her lips tingled, and it was the best feeling in the world. She'd been kissed by the man she loved.

Andrew grinned. "Come on, we'd best go." Brushing a gentle kiss across her forehead, he slipped an arm around her shoulder. "They'll be wondering where we are." As he winked at her, a tingle of delight ran through her body.

Slipping her arm around his waist, she leaned into him. "Maybe we won't ask anyone to come with us to the hospital."

He kissed the top of her head. "Good idea."

EYES WIDENED when Andrew announced to everyone that he and Brianna were driving to the hospital.

"You're not going out in this weather, surely?" Disbelief punctured David's thick voice.

"We'll be fine, Dad. I've driven in much worse."

"I know you have, son, but still… it's Christmas Eve."

Andrew placed his hand lightly on Brianna's shoulder. "Brianna wants to be there for Grace."

Grins formed on Lizzy's and Caitlin's faces. A flush crept up Brianna's neck and into her cheeks. There was no hiding it now.

"Well, take care, son. We don't want any more accidents."

"I will, Dad. Don't worry."

"Give our best to Grace," Lizzy said. "Tell her she needs to be home by morning or the children will be disappointed."

"We will."

They bid everyone good-bye and escaped out the side door, and were immediately blasted by a biting wind.

CHAPTER 11

*G*race clung to Ryan's hand as the rescuers placed her onto a stretcher. She steeled herself for the journey down the mountain. A helicopter would have been preferable, but as the wind was still gusting, the snowmobile was the only way down.

Fergus, a short, stout, ruddy-faced man dressed in high visibility rescue gear, assured her they'd take it slowly, and would make the ride as comfortable as possible. An ambulance would be waiting at the bottom to take her to the hospital.

Ryan sat close to her as the snowmobile began its descent. When the snowmobile became airborne and landed hard several times, Grace thought she would pass out as pain shot through her body, but they finally came to a stop. They'd made it.

As promised, an ambulance was waiting, along with Daniel and Caleb. Her brothers' faces were a welcome sight. The drive to the hospital took forever. Ryan told her it was because the road was slippery and they wanted to get there safely. That was fine with her... she was drifting into numbness now that the pain relief had kicked in.

Grace opened her eyes as the lights of Fort William flickered through the ambulance windows. "Are we almost there?" Her voice sounded tinny and far away in her ears.

Ryan smoothed her brow with his hand. "A few more minutes."

Her eyes fell shut again.

The sound of the ambulance door opening aroused her. The stretcher was lifted out and wheels snapped into place as it was lowered to the ground. Bright lights hurt her eyes as she was rushed inside. She tried to lift her hand to cover them, but her arms were secured in place. She began to panic, tried lifting her head, looked around. Then she remembered—she wasn't in prison, she was in the hospital.

Ryan spoke gently. "It's okay, Grace. You're safe."

~

BRIANNA SNUGGLED close to Andrew as he shoved the gear stick of his father's four-wheel-drive into first and headed down the rough track leading to the tiny highland village of Glen Brannie. She still couldn't believe he had kissed her. Reaching up, she pressed her fingers to her lips—there was no question about it. Her heart sang with delight, a warm glow filling her body as snow chains rattled and pine branches heavy with snow scraped against the vehicle.

Andrew drove in silence, concentrating on the road. The tyres skidded and the vehicle fishtailed as he made a run up a steep hill, but they made it out of the pine forest without any drama. Approaching the small village, an array of Christmas lights flashed from the roofs of old stone cottages, reminding her it was actually Christmas. The only shop in the village, a general store she knew well from her time living at the community, sold everything from bread and milk to all things Scottish, including home-made shortbread and tea-towels adorned with Scottish recipes and pictures of Ben Nevis and the Loch Ness Monster. The shop was closed, but a Christmas tree sat in the window, lights twinkly and cheery.

Brianna glanced at Andrew as he turned onto the wider road leading to Fort William, recently salted and gritted after the snowplough had been through. The clear-cut lines of his profile stood out against the moonlight now reflecting off the dark waters of Loch Linnhe. Her heart filled with warmth. He was a most handsome man.

When the lights of Fort William came into view, Andrew slowed to turn into the road leading to the hospital. He parked in the almost empty car park, not surprising since it was Christmas Eve. He offered his arm to help her along the slippery path leading to the entrance. It felt nice. As his hand closed over hers in a squeeze, a wave of contentment flowed through her.

When the automatic doors opened, the comforting sounds of *Silent Night* played through the hospital's speakers. A giant Christmas tree, decorated with colourful baubles, white and silver tinsel, and flashing lights, dominated the small waiting area. Daniel and Caleb sat on chairs against a wall. They looked up with mouths gaping. "We didn't expect to see you here." Danny stepped forward and hugged Brianna.

"It was a spur of the moment decision." She gave Andrew a coy look. "Andrew's suggestion."

"Well, Grace will be happy you've come."

"How is she? Can we see her?"

"The doctor's with her now, so we'll have to wait. She was in a lot of pain, but she's had some meds, so she should be feeling better soon."

"We were so worried..." Brianna choked out, pushing back the tears welling in her eyes.

Andrew wrapped his arm around her and rubbed her arm. Danny and Caleb both took notice, but she didn't care. It felt good being cared for by Andrew. And why wouldn't they be happy for her?

"I'll grab some tea." Caleb headed to the self-service drink dispenser.

"How did you get here?" Brianna asked Daniel. Sniffing, she reached into her pocket and drew out a tissue. If she could keep the conversation away from Grace and her injury, she might not break down and embarrass herself.

"A lift with one of the rescuers."

Of course. "Where's Ryan?" She looked around, having almost forgotten about him.

"In with Grace and the doctor. Come and sit down, Bibi." Danny gestured to the chairs he and Caleb had vacated.

Caleb handed her a polystyrene cup filled with hot, sweet tea. She brought it to her mouth and took a sip. It was just what she needed.

"The children wanted to come in and sing Christmas Carols to the patients." Brianna forced herself to chat.

Danny chuckled. "Of course they did."

"Will Grace make it home for Christmas?" Brianna's voice quieted as she met Danny's gaze.

He released a slow breath and skimmed his hand through his hair. His eyes were watery and slightly red. "Not sure. We'll know more once the doctor comes out."

Brianna grimaced. That wasn't what she wanted to hear. The children would be devastated if Grace wasn't there in the morning. They really needed that miracle.

"Let's go and visit the other patients while we wait. Sing some carols," Andrew suggested.

His happy face cheered her, pulling her out of her self-pity.

Danny rubbed his hands together. "Not so sure about the singing, but yes, visiting the patients is a grand idea."

"Will we be allowed?" Brianna asked.

"Of course. It's Christmas Eve, and besides, I know the sister on duty." Danny winked.

Brianna shook her head. Of course Danny would know the sister on duty. Danny knew everyone.

After he checked with the sister, who said they were more than welcome to visit the patients, Brianna followed the three men into the women's ward. The foursome offered Christmas greetings to five older ladies who were spending Christmas in hospital. Danny knew four of them, and they were very pleased to see him.

Andrew had just finished leading a surprisingly melodious rendition of *The First Noel*, when Ryan found them. Like Danny, he too looked tired, but his grin was so wide it nearly slid off his face. "They're letting her go home."

Danny gave him a bear hug. "That's great news."

Brianna hugged him too, pushing back relieved tears.

"She'll be ready shortly." Ryan spoke to Brianna. "I didn't know you were coming in."

"We wanted to be here for her."

"She'll be glad to see you." He smiled and then turned his head as a nurse pushing Grace in a wheelchair stopped at the entrance to the ward.

They bid the ladies a merry Christmas and then left to approach the nurse. With her arm in a sling and still in her ski clothes, Grace looked a little worse for wear, but she still managed a weak smile.

Brianna gave her a gentle hug, taking care not to hurt her injured shoulder. Despite her intention to be strong, tears sprang from her eyes. "I'm so glad you're coming home."

"So am I, trust me. It wasn't easy convincing them I'm okay —they wanted to keep me in. Anyway, let's get out of here." She looked up at the nurse and thanked her. "I'll be all right from here, thanks."

"No, I'll push you to your car. No argument, thank you."

"I'll get the car," Andrew said.

When Andrew left, Ryan whispered to Brianna, "So, what's going on between you two?"

She stiffened. "Nothing." Her voice was small but defensive.

Ryan chuckled. "Yeah, right."

Grace reached out her good hand and smacked Ryan playfully. "Leave Bibi alone. I think it's lovely." She reached out her hand to squeeze Brianna's.

With her brothers, brother-in-law and sister in the car on the way home, Brianna sat further away from Andrew than she had on the drive there, but every now and then she shot him a glance, and each time she did, her heart did a little skip.

CHAPTER 12

$\mathcal{I}$t was nearing midnight when they arrived back at Elim Community. The storm had completely cleared, and instead of dark, angry clouds and a howling gale, stars shone down from an unusually clear sky. When Andrew helped Brianna out of the car and offered his arm, she was tempted to suggest a stroll to the loch, but it was so cold her nose was running. Instead, she pulled her coat tighter and leaned in close to him.

Ryan carefully carried Grace the short distance to the house. Lizzy and Caitlin greeted Daniel and Caleb at the door, quickly ushering them inside. Andrew slipped his arm around Brianna's shoulder as they followed.

The grandfather clock struck midnight as Andrew closed the door. They were alone in the foyer. He drew her close, the tenderness of his gaze sending her pulse racing. "There might not be any mistletoe, but I think it's time for another kiss." His breath was warm and moist as his lips feather-touched hers.

Brianna's knees weakened with longing. She still could not believe this was happening. Brianna O'Connor, kissed by the most gorgeous man ever. Unheard of. But it was real. She drank in the sweetness of his kiss, lost in the magic of the moment. "Merry Christmas, lassie." Gazing into her eyes, he tenderly traced the line of her cheekbone and jaw with his finger.

She smiled dreamily into his eyes. "And to you, Andrew."

Lowering his head, his lips had just touched hers again when, in front of them, someone cleared his throat. "Come on, you two. You can't stay there all night." Danny's voice held amusement as he stood in the hallway with his arm draped around Lizzy's shoulder.

A flush crept into Brianna's face—she hadn't heard them sneak up.

"Leave them alone, Daniel." Lizzy spoke quietly as she looked up at him. "We're off to bed... no doubt the children will be up early. Good night, and merry Christmas."

"Merry Christmas to you both, as well. And no, we won't stay here all night. Don't you worry about that," Andrew replied.

"Good night, then." Lizzy smiled before dragging Daniel away.

Brianna knew she should go to bed, but she didn't want this night to end. Even with Grace's accident, it had been the best day she'd ever had, so when Andrew asked if she'd like a hot chocolate, she didn't think twice. "And shortbread?"

"Whatever you like." He lifted his hand, tucking a lock of hair behind her ear before popping a kiss on her lips and leading her to the kitchen.

Brianna sat on a stool and watched as Andrew made the most amazing hot chocolate ever. Rich, velvety and topped with whipped cream, she thought she'd died and gone to heaven.

"Like it?" He angled his head.

"Love it."

"Let's find somewhere cosy to sit."

"Okay."

He led her into the drawing room where he re-stoked the fire, put on some quiet Christmas music, and joined her on the couch. "I'm not in any hurry to go to bed." He slipped his arm around her shoulder and kissed the side of her head.

She leaned into him. "Neither am I."

"We might see Santa come down the chimney."

Brianna giggled. "He's not real, remember. Besides, he might get burned if he comes down this one."

"You have a point."

"Tell me more about your travels."

"What do you want to know?"

"Everything."

"It might take all night."

"I don't care."

"In that case…"

For the next few hours, Andrew told Brianna about all the amazing places he'd travelled to, but the one she was most interested in was the walk he'd done in Spain.

"So what made it so special?" she asked him as the clock stuck three.

"I was at a low point in my life. A girl I'd been with for a few years had just ditched me for someone else, and I was looking for something." He released a slow breath as he stared into the fire. "I felt empty. I could have come home, but I wasn't ready for that. I'd heard about the walk, and something about it appealed, so I decided to do it."

He ran his finger around the top of his mug. "I was in Barcelona working in a restaurant, so I packed up and headed for *Saint Jean Pied de Port* and began walking." Pausing, he turned to look at her. "It wasn't so much the scenery, although some of it was awesome, or even the people I met along the way. It was the time I spent alone, just walking, that made it special."

"I've never done anything like that. Hiked on my own."

Andrew squeezed Brianna's hand, rubbing his thumb gently over her skin. "It wasn't easy. I had to push myself often, but I learned the most about myself at the places that were most challenging. That was when God got through to me." He smiled. "Every night I read a chapter of the Bible and asked Him to be real to me, because even though I'd grown up in a Christian home, I didn't *know* Him, I just knew *about* Him. And every day I prayed David's prayer from Psalm 63 verse one: '*O God, You are my God; I shall seek You earnestly; My soul thirsts for You, my flesh yearns for You, In a dry and weary land where there is no water.*'

"And one day, somewhere high in the mountains of *O Cebreiro* when I was thirsty, hot and tired, with blisters upon blisters on my feet, God spoke to my heart, and I knew then, beyond a shadow of a doubt, that He was real. I sat on a rock, all alone apart from some bleating sheep, the air so clean it hurt to breathe, and something moved in my heart. I began to cry. I fell on my knees and gave my life to God there and then."

Brianna let his words sink in a few moments before she replied. "That's amazing. I can understand your experience, because mine was similar. Something happened inside me the day your mother led me to the Lord, and any doubt I had that God cared was blown away. I knew that God loved me and wanted me for His own. It still amazes me that He did that. I was the worst person ever."

Andrew shook his head. "No, you weren't."

"I felt like it. I couldn't understand for a while why He'd bother with me. I was a nobody. A drug addict. A thief. But he loved me enough to send Jesus to die for me." Brianna pulled out a tissue and dabbed her eyes. "It still blows me away."

"Me too. His love is amazing, and it must break His heart that so many shun Him, because He just wants to give them a new life. A fresh start. I know it breaks my heart."

"Mine, too." Brianna thought of all the rape victims she'd shared her faith with, but how few welcomed God's message of hope and love. They couldn't understand His love, and yet, if they only admitted their need, she knew that God would take their hand and give them a much better life.

She leaned her head against Andrew's chest and he tenderly stroked her hair. She sat up abruptly when Alana crossed her mind. "I'd really like to pray for Alana. I think God's working in her heart, but she knows so little about Him, and she's hurting badly. I've been praying for the right time to share with her, but it never seems to happen."

"Sure." He smiled warmly. "That's a great idea."

ANDREW BOWED his head and listened to Brianna pray. Her voice, so soft, so caring. Just like everything about her. He'd fallen for her, and it seemed she'd fallen for him, but would that change once she knew the truth? Like it or not, he needed to tell her. He should have told her already.

Brianna said *Amen* and raised her head. In the light of the embers, her eyes flickered and shone. He had to tell her. Taking her hand, he stroked her soft skin with his thumb. "I... I need to tell you something. I don't know how to say it, so I'll just blurt it out."

Brianna's eyes widened. "What is it, Andrew?"

A knot twisted in his stomach. Not even his parents knew. He'd been planning on telling them, but hadn't found the right time, but he couldn't keep putting it off. He ran his hand through his hair. Gosh, he was still coming to terms with it himself. Still digesting the news that had thrown him for six only weeks before. He still wondered if it was true or not, or if he was just being set up. *Used.* But somehow, he knew it was true. He had a son. An eleven-year old son. *Andy.*

He braced himself and gazed into Brianna's eyes. "Brianna, you're everything I've ever wanted in a woman... I love your heart, the way you care. I love your gentleness, your depth of character. But I can't lead you on without telling you that..." His gaze dropped to his lap. Was this the right time to tell her? Was it premature? Presumptuous? Should he wait? If he told her, it could mean she'd run a mile, and he wouldn't blame her. Or it could galvanise their relationship when maybe it shouldn't. *What if she decided to date him because he had a son, compensating for the one she'd lost?* Would he ever know? *Would it matter?*

He had to trust his instincts. His heart. Somehow, he knew Brianna was genuine. She wouldn't abuse the situation. Besides, he'd already started the conversation and couldn't very well drop it now. He lifted his eyes slowly, meeting hers. "I have an eleven-year-old son."

Hazel eyes held his without blinking; the only sound was the hissing from a log that crackled in the fire. Brief moments passed. He tried to smooth his face into an emotionless mask, allowing her time to digest this news.

She finally blinked. "Where is he?" Her voice was soft, just like her eyes.

"With his mother."

"Tell me about him."

Andrew closed his eyes. Images of a sandy-haired boy who bore his own facial features flitted through his mind. Yes, Andy was definitely his son. He opened his eyes and looked up. "Remember that girl I mentioned?"

"The one who ditched you?"

He nodded. "She contacted me a month ago. Came to the restaurant, in fact. She'd seen a feature article in a newspaper with my photo, so she said. She asked for me, and to cut a long story short, we had a drink after work, and that's when she told me about Andy."

"You didn't know until then?"

"No." He held her gaze.

"Wow. Why now, after all this time?"

"She's sick. Dying." An ache pierced his chest at saying the words aloud. "She's got cancer."

"Cancer? That's terrible."

"Yes." He could see Brianna's mind ticking.

"So, what did she want?"

Blood surged through his veins. "She wants me to look after Andy."

Brianna's gaze remained steady. *What was she thinking?* She angled her head. Moistened her lips. Took her time. She looked deeply into his eyes. "How do you feel about that?" Her voice was gentle. Caring. Non-judgmental. He could imagine her asking a similar question of her rape victims.

He relaxed and answered honestly. "Excited. Scared. I know nothing about raising a kid."

Her face broke into a wide smile and she clasped his hands. "But you're great with them. And they love you."

Andrew let out a nervous chuckle. "That may be, but I'm sure it would be different being a full-time parent."

"Have you met him?"

He nodded. "Just before I came up here."

"Do your parents know?"

He grimaced.

"I take that as a no."

"I haven't known how to tell them."

"I'm sure they'll be thrilled to have a grandson."

"Maybe." He raked a hand through his hair, blinking rapidly.

"It would be a great Christmas gift for them."

"I should tell them."

"Yes." She held his gaze.

"I've been praying about it non-stop," Andrew admitted. "There's still a lot to work through, but yes, I think I'll take him." He'd said it. *Finally.* And it felt right.

"You'll make a great father, Andrew."

Tears pricked his eyes. Until recently, he'd never thought about having children. Yes, it was true he loved kids, but he'd never had full-time responsibility for any. Never pictured himself being a father, *especially to an eleven-year old.* Andy would be a teenager soon. *What did he know about raising a teenager?* Andy seemed like a good kid, but he'd have issues. What kid didn't? And how would he cope when Shelley died, because die she would, and soon, unless God performed a miracle. But Shelley didn't believe, so not much chance of that happening. He brushed his eyes and gave Brianna a grateful smile. "Thanks."

He wanted to ask her how she felt about the news and if this would change anything between them. Not that there was anything between them, *yet.* Just a few kisses that might not have meant anything to her. Although he sensed they had. Brianna might have been swept up in emotion. He sensed she'd never been kissed before, at least not in the way he'd kissed her, but despite that, she seemed to genuinely care for him. It had been wrong to put her in this position. He should never have let his attraction to her get the better of him. But it had happened, and now here she was, finding out he had a son he was about to take full responsibility for. *Would it change anything?*

He took her hand again. "I know we've only just met, but I really like you, Brianna." She started to speak, but he shooshed her. "Please let me finish."

She nodded.

"I don't know how you feel about dating a man with an eleven-year old son he doesn't really know, but I'd love it if you'd give it a shot. But I'll understand if you'd rather not have anything more to do with me."

A few beats passed before she spoke. "Are you asking me to go out with you? To be your girlfriend?"

"Yes..." Andrew sucked in a breath. Was he about to get the best Christmas gift ever?

"Of course I will!" Her eyes lit up as she threw her arms around his neck.

"Even with an eleven-year old appendage?"

"Even with an eleven-year old appendage."

Their eyes locked. He couldn't believe this was happening. He didn't want to think too far ahead, but an image of the three of them together filled his mind, and deep peace filled his heart.

He lowered his head and was about to kiss her when he heard a noise. He raised his head and chuckled. Four small bodies, all wearing colourful flannelette pyjamas, stood about a foot from them.

Brianna also chuckled, amusement flickering in her eyes as she held out her arms to them. "What are you four doing up?"

"Seeing if Santa's come," Clare said, hugging her precious stuffed elephant close to her chest as she slid onto Brianna's lap.

"We haven't seen him yet, but he probably won't visit while we're here and awake. We might need to go back to bed so he'll come."

Dillon began to speak, but Brianna gave him a warning look.

"Is Auntie Grace home?" Clare asked.

Brianna pulled her close and smoothed the little girl's hair. "Yes, Auntie Grace is home."

"That's good. I prayed she would be okay."

"And God heard you." Brianna kissed the top of her head.

The three boys moved to the fire and one of them started prodding it with the poker.

Andrew quickly hopped off the couch. "Best not to stir it up if we're going back to bed."

"Can't we stay up?" Dillon asked. "You're up."

"Yes, but we were just about to go to bed."

"No you weren't. You were just about to kiss Auntie Brianna."

Ruffling Dillon's hair, Andrew stifled a laugh. "Maybe I was, but we need to get to bed now or we might all get into trouble."

Standing, he took Dillon's and James' hands, while Brianna placed Clare on the floor and took her hand along with Quinn's, and they all tiptoed up the stairs, trying not to make any noise. After delivering Dillon, James and Clare to their rooms, Brianna stood on tippy toes and placed a kiss of promise on Andrew's lips before leading Quinn into the room she shared with him and Alana.

As Andrew walked back into his parents' wing along the long hallway, his feet felt lighter and his heart overflowed with hope and anticipation. It seemed God hadn't just given him a son, but He might also have given him someone to share his life with. He was getting ahead of himself, but so far, this was the best Christmas ever.

CHAPTER 13

*S*lipping into bed, Brianna pulled the duvet around her neck until she was snuggly and warm. Her heart sang. Blissfully happy, she felt fully alive, *and awake*. Sleep was needed, because no doubt the children would wake again soon, and she didn't want to miss the joy and excitement of Christmas morning. But how could she sleep?

Andrew had a son. *A son!* That's what he'd been hiding from her. What kind of Christmas would young Andy be having? The last one with his mother... Brianna's heart ached for him. If anyone knew what it was like to lose your mother as a pre-teen, she did, and she wouldn't wish it upon anyone. The poor little boy... he must feel so alone and scared.

But filling her thoughts more than that, was that Andrew had asked *her* to be his girlfriend. *To date him!*

Suddenly, reality hit her. *If* things progressed with Andrew, and *if* he went ahead with his plans of caring for Andy full-time, then she could become the mother of an eleven-year old.

Perspiration dampened her body. Throwing off the duvet, she lay flat on her back, gazing at the ceiling. It was one thing to have fallen in love when she'd never expected to, but completely another when it might lead to being an instant mother. What did she know about raising a child? Maybe it was too much. Maybe she should end the relationship while she could. Before it got too hard.

The more Brianna thought about it, the more her mind spun. How could she let Andrew go now? But how could she continue? She released a huge sigh. Prayer was needed. If this was what God wanted, He'd give her whatever skills were required.

Sitting up, she pulled her bed-jacket around her shoulders, bowed her head and prayed quietly, asking God for guidance and wisdom. She also prayed for Andrew, and for Andy. Lastly, she prayed for Shelley, that in her final days before passing, she might open her heart to God's love, and would experience His peace in her life.

Resting in the knowledge that God would give her the direction and guidance she needed, Brianna finally drifted off to sleep.

SOMETIME LATER, her eyes snapped open when little hands shook her.

"Auntie Bianna, wake up. It's Christmas." She just made out Quinn's face in the dark room.

Quickly sitting, she threaded her fingers through her hair and glanced at the clock on the bedside table. *Six o'clock.* Not bad. She must have gotten a few hours' sleep.

Moments later, a knock sounded on her door, followed by Danny's cheery voice. "Everybody up. Merry Christmas!" He sounded as excited as a five-year old.

"Is your mummy awake?" Brianna clicked on the bedside lamp and smiled at Quinn.

He shook his head.

"Why don't you see if you can wake her? I'll grab my gown then I'll come help. Oh, and by the way, merry Christmas!" She pulled the little boy close and gave him a big hug.

He ran off to wake Alana, although Brianna suspected he might need help. Alana certainly was a heavy sleeper.

Slipping out of bed, she shivered and quickly grabbed her thick, quilted gown and slippers. A quick glance in the mirror told her she needed more sleep. Running her hands through her hair again, she tied it back loosely, then ducked into the bathroom before stepping into Alana's side of the room. Alana was stirring and opened her eyes as Brianna approached. Quinn just stood there looking at his mother, melting Brianna's heart.

"Merry Christmas, Alana," Brianna said softly as she smiled at her sister, recalling the prayer she'd prayed just hours before, that today Alana would experience God's love in her life.

Alana yawned, stretched, then pulled Quinn in for a hug. "Merry Christmas, Quinny." As she kissed the top of his dark, messy hair, she returned Brianna's smile. "And merry Christmas to you."

"Can we go downstairs, Mummy?" Quinn hopped up and down like a bunny.

"Yes, Quinny. Just let Mummy get dressed. I'll only be a

moment." She plopped him on the bed and then grabbed her gown and visited the bathroom.

Once both Alana and Brianna had changed out of their night attire and into warm, fleecy pants and thick sweaters, the three of them headed downstairs, drawn by the happy sounds of the other children.

Danny, Lizzy and the children were already in the drawing room where the fire that Andrew had put out only hours before was now blazing. Quinn let go Alana's hand and skidded onto the floor to sit beside James and Dillon. Clare sat on Danny's lap.

"Merry Christmas," Danny and Lizzy said in unison. Brianna leaned down and gave them both a hug before sitting with Alana on the same couch she'd sat on with Andrew only hours before.

Andrew wasn't there yet, but every time someone entered, she looked up expectantly. When Grace and Ryan entered, a hush fell over the room. Grace's arm was in a sling, and several bruises on her face had darkened. Clare jumped up and wrapped her arms around Grace's middle. "Merry Christmas, Auntie Grace. Is your arm sore?"

Grace let out a small laugh. Brianna knew her sister was fascinated by Clare's attraction to her, but neither she nor Grace had any idea what had caused the little girl to single Grace out as her favourite auntie. Whatever the reason, Grace loved it. And she loved Clare. They had a special relationship. Strange, really, because Grace had never shown much interest in having children of her own. She bent down and hugged Clare as best as she could with one arm. "It's just a little sore, but I'm okay. Thanks, sweetie."

"Can I sit with you?" Clare's little voice was so adorable. Grace face lit up. "You sure can."

The chatter in the room returned, escalating when Lizzy's parents, Brendan, Shawn, Aislin, Joel, Rosemary, David, Caleb and the girls all arrived. But no Caitlin, *and no Andrew*. Brianna tried to still her thumping heart. Just the memory of his kisses made her blush. She couldn't wait to see him, but then there was still the question of Andy... *what if God said no?* She prayed that wouldn't be the case. Somehow it felt right. *But where was he?*

Moments later, when the children were getting restless and wanting to open their presents, the door opened and Andrew and Caitlin entered carrying trays of steaming coffee, croissants and pastries. Brianna's gaze immediately went to his, and when they met, her heart-rate accelerated.

He began offering coffee to everybody, but when he stopped in front of her, joy bubbled inside her. How could a man like Andrew McKinnon have fallen for her? Even though he had a past, and now a present that included a son, he was everything Brianna had never known she'd wanted until now. Her heart pounded as she gave him a shy smile and took a coffee from the tray.

When he walked on, Alana whispered in Brianna's ear. "Did I just see something between you two?"

Brianna couldn't hide it if she tried. She nodded, knowing her eyes shone, but not trusting herself to speak.

"I thought so. That's wonderful, Brianna. I'm happy for you."

She squeezed Alana's hand. "Thank you."

"He's a good catch."

"He is…"

As Andrew offered the coffee tray to his parents, Brianna wondered when he'd tell them about Andy, *their grandson.* Would they be excited, or would they be disappointed? If she knew them as well as she thought she did, they'd welcome the boy into their family with loving arms.

Andrew put the empty tray down on the side buffet, grabbed a coffee for himself, along with a croissant, and then sat on the floor at Brianna's feet. They shared a smile as he tilted his head, and then she sat back and watched with amusement as Danny distributed all the presents, with Dillon and James acting as little helpers.

The delight in the children's faces and voices was contagious, and the atmosphere in the room was such a happy one. Just like Christmas should be. Once all the presents had been opened, and the room was littered with wrapping paper, toys, games, clothing and other assorted gifts, Danny announced that following breakfast, a short church service would be held in the chapel, and he hoped everyone would attend.

Brianna turned to Alana, trying to gauge her reaction. *Nothing.* She needed to say something. With firm resolve, she met Alana's gaze. "I'd love you to come to the service, Alana? Will you? Quinny will enjoy it. Danny's got things planned for the children."

Alana shrugged. "I guess so, although I'm not really a church-goer."

Brianna squeezed her hand. "It doesn't matter. I think it'll be fun." She turned her head and rolled her eyes. What was she saying? *Fun?* Church wasn't normally fun, but maybe today it would be. Especially if Danny was leading the service.

Andrew stood and offered his hand to help her up. Brianna still had to pinch herself that this had happened. It was like she forgot, but then when she saw him, or they touched, a wave of warmth swept over her, reminding her that something indeed was happening between them.

When he returned to the kitchen, where no doubt he was concocting something amazing for breakfast, Brianna helped clean up the mess. As she shoved the last of the paper into a huge garbage bag, Grace caught Brianna's eye and patted the spot beside her on the couch. She adjusted her position and looked Brianna in the eye. "So, are you going to tell me?" Grace raised a brow, a grin on her face.

'Tell you what?"

"Come on Bibi, you can't hide anything from me, you know that."

Grace was right. They'd shared everything from the time they were young. Nothing was hidden between them. Besides, by the grin on her face, Grace already knew. Brianna let out a small chuckle and glanced at the ceiling. "I think you already know."

Grace's face lit up. "I'm so happy for you, Bibi. He seems like a good man."

Brianna nodded. If she could talk to anyone about 'the complication', it would be Grace. "Yes, but don't tell anyone..." She leaned closer and lowered her voice. "He has an eleven-year old son."

Grace's forehead creased. "Is that a problem?"

Brianna's shoulders sagged and she looked down at her hands. "I'm not sure." Lifting her head, she met Grace's uneasy gaze. "Andrew only found out about him a month ago, but the boy's mother is dying, and she wants Andrew to take him."

"Oh." For once, Grace seemed lost for words. Moments passed. The fire crackled. One of the children laughed. Brianna could see Grace's mind working. Finally, she spoke. "And is he going to take him?"

"I think so."

"How do you feel about that?"

"I've prayed about it."

"And?"

"I don't know yet, but I think I'm okay with it." Shrugging, Brianna fidgeted with her hands. "It's early days, anyway."

"Yes, but I've seen the way you look at each other. I can tell." Her eyes grew dreamy. "It was the same for Ryan and me. There was something special, different, and you just know. I can see it in you two."

"Really?" Brianna thought she might cry from happiness.

Grace nodded and tucked a strand of hair behind Brianna's ear.

"I can't believe all this has happened."

With her good arm, Grace drew her close and stroked her hair. "Bibi, God only wants good things for us, and I think this might be His good thing for you."

Brianna squeezed her eyes shut. It was almost too much... all those years of heartache, and more recently, the years of working with rape victims but not really living a life of joy and fun. Although she was so grateful that God had given her new life, and she was content, but if she were honest, she longed to be loved by someone special as well. Someone other than her siblings and friends. She'd accepted that might never happen, and she'd been scared of getting close to anyone. But now that love was a possibility, she was delighted, albeit, in shock.

"I think you'll be a great mum."

That did it. Tears streamed down Brianna's cheeks. Grace handed her a tissue. Brianna blew her nose. "Thank you."

"I mean it, Bibi. I think it's great." Grace leaned closer. "Can I tell you my secret now?" Her face lit up.

"You have a secret?" What was Grace hiding?

Grace's smile widened. "Don't worry—it's nothing bad. Ryan and I are expecting a baby."

Brianna's eyes popped. "You're not!"

"We are!"

"I didn't think you wanted children."

"Until I met Ryan, I didn't. Then everything changed. True love can do that for a person."

Brianna threw her arms around Grace, taking care not to hurt her sore shoulder. "That's fantastic news, Grace. Congratulations." Drawing back, a thought occurred to her. "Yesterday... the fall... is everything okay?"

"Yes, praise God. I'm perfect except for the collarbone and shoulder."

"I'm so sorry, Grace. If I hadn't gone skiing, you wouldn't have been worried about me and gone out looking for us."

"Don't say that, Bibi. It's all good."

"But it could have ended badly."

"It didn't, so no more. Okay?"

Brianna gave her a grateful smile. "Okay. So, who knows about the baby?"

"Only you."

"Oh. Okay, I won't say anything." Briana lowered her voice.

"We're planning on announcing it at lunch."

Brianna smiled again. "Everyone will be excited. I won't say anything until then."

"Thanks." Grace hugged her again. "We'd better go in for breakfast before it's all eaten. That man of yours is cooking something special, so I hear."

Brianna giggled. *Man of hers?* She liked the sound of that!

CHAPTER 14

*W*ith Caitlin acting as apprentice chef, Andrew had indeed prepared a special Christmas breakfast. French toast with mixed berries and whipped cream, pancakes with blueberry-plum syrup, and the tastiest little quiches Brianna had ever eaten. She patted her stomach as she thought how much weight she might put on if Andrew kept cooking like this.

After a very jolly breakfast and a quick clean-up, Danny gave a reminder about the service. Everyone, including Brendan, Shawn, Aislin and Joel, and Alana, said they'd be there.

After promising Alana she'd walk with her to the chapel, Brianna hung back in the kitchen and helped Andrew with the final clean-up. Andrew slipped his arms around her waist and gave her a slow kiss. "I've been wanting to do that all morning." His breath was warm and sweet and filled her with longing.

"Have you had any sleep?" she asked.

"No…" He kissed her again. "Too much on my mind."

Brianna pulled back. "Like telling your parents about Andy?"

"How did you guess?"

She shrugged. "That's got to be the biggest thing on your mind right now. So, when are you going to tell them?"

His shoulders slumped. "After church."

"I'm sure they'll be fine once they get over the initial shock."

"I hope so." He glanced at the clock on the wall. "We'd best go or we'll be late."

"I promised to walk with Alana. Save me a seat?" The prospect of sitting beside him in church filled Brianna with joy and anticipation. If their relationship was to develop, God had to be their focus, and what better day to start than Christmas Day?

"Yes, but hurry," he said. A thrill of excitement raced through her when he lowered his head and brushed his lips over hers. Would she ever get used to this?

"I will." She gazed into his eyes for a moment longer before tearing herself from his arms.

BRIANNA TOOK the steps two at a time, praying that Alana hadn't changed her mind. She smiled to herself when she reached the room. Quinn was seated on Alana's bed, hair brushed, face wiped, and wearing the new set of clothes Aislin and Joel had given him for Christmas—dark blue corduroy trousers and a hand-knitted red sweater. He looked adorable. And Alana had applied a little make-up... amazing how much difference it made to her appearance. Brianna was pleased Alana wanted to look her best for church. Not that it mattered. With the amount of snow they'd had, most likely it would only be family attending, as well as David, Rosemary and Andrew. But the fact that she'd taken care with herself heartened Brianna.

"You look nice, Alana." She flashed a warm smile and then squatted in front of Quinn, getting down to his level. "And you look so cute in those new clothes, little Quinny."

His face beamed. "Auntie Ash made them for me."

"She's a very clever auntie."

He nodded as he inspected the trucks and tippers Aislin had knitted into each wrist band. She'd obviously taken a great deal of care.

Straightening, Brianna glanced in the mirror. A little make-up was needed to camouflage her lack of sleep. "I'll just be a minute." Darting into the shared bathroom, she smoothed her hair and brushed her teeth, then threw on some blusher, a light coat of mascara, and a quick lick of lipstick. That would have to do.

"Ready?" she asked, re-entering the bedroom.

Alana nodded, took Quinn's hand, and they followed Brianna out the door.

THE SMALL CHAPEL sat on the far side of the main Elim Community building. Built of stone, it had once been a barn, but quite a few years ago it had been renovated and made into a simple place of worship, and now it even had stained glass windows. Although mainly intended for the students and staff of the Community, people now came from miles around. The small church's reputation for preaching God's word without compromise had spread over the years.

The chapel was more than half full—people had braved the weather after all. Brianna's eyes searched for Andrew, and when she caught sight of his tawny-gold hair her heart skipped a beat. Would she ever be able to look at him without having palpitations? Somehow, she doubted it.

She ushered Alana and Quinn forward, directing them to the pew on the left, midway down the small chapel, where Andrew sat with his parents. Alana motioned for her to sit beside Andrew, while she and Quinn took the spots nearest the aisle. When Andrew slipped his hand into hers, squeezing gently, a thrill raced up her spine. There had been many times when she'd looked at Danny and Lizzy and Grace and Ryan sitting close to each other in church that she wondered what it was like to sit with someone special while worshipping God together. She was about to find out, but so far, she liked it.

Danny and Lizzy and the others had done a great job of decorating the chapel. A nativity scene, complete with a small make-shift barn, hay, cows, sheep, the three wise men, and the baby Jesus with Mary and Joseph, took pride of place at the front of the chapel. Dillon played *Joy to the World* on the piano while Lizzy stood and turned the pages. Although he barely reached the pedals, he played brilliantly.

The other children sat in the front pew beside Grace, Ryan and Danny. When Dillon finished playing, Danny stood and welcomed everyone, inviting the congregation to stand and sing the carol that expressed the joy of Christmas.

Brianna glanced at Andrew and smiled before turning to Alana.

She had picked Quinn up and placed him on her hip.

Brianna leaned closer. "Are you okay?"

Alana nodded, a small smile lifting the corners of her mouth.

"Let me know if you'd like a break."

"Thanks."

Brianna inched closer to Andrew and began singing.

The service was everything she had expected and more. Danny and Lizzy had a special gift when it came to running a service, and they had planned songs and a short activity just for the children in which they all played a part, even Quinn. Caleb and Caitlin's girls took turns reading the Bible verses, telling the story of Jesus' birth in the manger, and there was lots of singing. When Danny stood at the lectern to start the sermon, Brianna shifted in her seat, growing a little anxious. Normally she loved listening to Danny preach, but with Alana beside her, and Brendan, Shawn and the others not far away, she hoped he'd make it short and to the point.

When he started by promising not to speak for long, Brianna breathed a sigh of relief and relaxed, but prayed silently that God would speak through him to everyone there. Danny had never formally trained as a preacher, but he spoke from the heart, and that, combined with his easy-going nature, meant that whenever he spoke, it was entertaining but meaningful, and God used him to touch peoples' hearts. Brianna prayed that today would be no different.

"Christmas is just the best time of year, isn't it?" he began. "And this Christmas it's even better having all my family here. To me, that's what the message of Christmas is all about... *connecting*. God connecting with man, people connecting with people, families connecting with each other. Love, acceptance, new beginnings, *hope*. We can all do with that, especially hope. God sent His only son, Jesus, to earth as a baby for just that reason... to give hope and a future to all those who believe."

As Danny continued to speak, Alana brushed her damp face with the back of her hand. Brianna reached out, placing her hand gently against Alana's shoulder while sending up another prayer. God was touching Alana's heart, and Brianna couldn't have been happier.

Danny finished his short sermon by asking everyone to bow their heads while he prayed. From the corner of her eye, Brianna noticed Alana sniffle as she closed her eyes. Brianna slipped an arm around her shoulders, pulling her close while Danny prayed.

Fresh tears continued to slide down Alana's cheeks. When Danny finished praying and everyone rose to sing 'Hark, the Herald Angels Sing', Brianna offered to take Quinn. The little boy clung to her while staring at his mother with his thumb in his mouth.

As the carol ended, Brianna leaned closer to Andrew and whispered, "I'm going to stay here with Alana for a while. Okay?" Their eyes held for a second, and she knew he understood.

Nodding, Andrew held his arms out to Quinn. "Come with me?"

The little boy quickly climbed across, wrapping his arms around Andrew's neck.

Brianna smiled her thanks. "I'll catch you soon." For a moment, she thought Andrew might lean across and kiss her, but she was very relieved when he didn't. They hadn't formally told his parents they were dating yet, although she assumed they'd guessed. Andrew and his parents left the pew in the opposite direction, leaving her with Alana.

Memories of Rosemary sitting with her not that long ago flashed through Brianna's mind. God's first touch on a life was such a precious time... inexplicable, but real, nonetheless. She sat quietly with her arm around Alana's shoulder, giving time for her sister to compose herself before saying anything. When Alana raised her head slightly, Brianna searched her eyes. "Are you all right, Alana? Would you like to talk?"

Alana nodded, sniffing.

"God's affecting you inside, isn't He?"

Alana nodded again.

"I'd love to pray for you, and then maybe we can spend some time chatting. Would you like that?"

Another nod. Another sniff.

Bowing her head, Brianna paused before beginning. Her heart was filled with gratitude that this moment had finally arrived, and she didn't want to spoil it. She took a slow breath and began in a quiet voice. "Dear God, thank You for my precious sister, Alana. You know what's going on inside her, the hurt she's experienced, the disappointments, the lack of hope. Thank You for gently reaching out to her, showing her how much You love her, how precious she is to You. Lord God, I pray that today, as we celebrate the birth of your son, Jesus, who came into the world so that all who believe in Him can have eternal life, I pray that You'll touch her in a real way, and that she might open her heart to You and to Your healing. Lord God, I pray special blessings upon her life, and I thank You so much for her precious little boy. Bless Quinn, dear Lord, and may he also come to know You. I ask all these things in Jesus' precious name, Amen."

Brianna wiped her own eyes as she raised her head and gave Alana a big hug.

Sniffing, and with eyes moist, Alana hugged her back. "Thank you."

"You're more than welcome."

Alana blew her nose. "I've... I've never really believed in God too much. I guess I always assumed He was there, but never thought He was of any use in my life. But since being here, with you, and Danny and Lizzy, and all the others, I can see that He's changed you all, and I think I want what you've got." Tears streamed down her cheeks again.

"That's the best thing I've heard all day." Brianna handed Alana a clean tissue. "It's really simple. You just have to be sorry for all the things you've done wrong, and then claim the forgiveness that Jesus brought when he died on the cross, and then ask Him to come and live in your heart. It sounds a bit mysterious, but Jesus, being perfect, took on the sins of the whole world when He died on the cross, so that anyone who believes can be made clean in God's sight and have new life. It's a lot to take in, and we can talk about it more, but that's basically it."

"It sounds great, but I think I need to understand a little better before I make a decision."

"That's perfectly fine. It's a big thing, and you shouldn't do it lightly, but having an open heart is the first step. That's all He asks of you, to open your heart and your mind, and He'll gently lead you to Himself when you're ready. But let me tell you, when you do, it's like a whole new world opening up. I couldn't believe how free I felt after all those years of drug addiction and self-hate. God has made such a difference in my life, and He can in yours, too."

"I really want to know more. I'm tired of living like I do." Alana blinked back tears again.

Pulling her close, Brianna rubbed Alana's back, rocking her like a baby. "I know. Believe me, I know."

They sat there for several more minutes before Brianna straightened. "We can chat more later, okay?"

"Yes, thanks." Alana dabbed her nose and nodded.

"Let's grab a coffee."

"Sounds great."

Brianna stood first and helped Alana up. Although the chapel was now empty, a special sense of God's presence filled the air.

CHAPTER 15

*A*ndrew followed his parents out of the chapel with Quinn perched on his hip and shot a backwards glance to Brianna. His heart was with her, but Alana would be more comfortable chatting with her sister alone. *Besides, there was that talk with his parents.* He walked behind them, gathering his courage. How would his parents take the news that they had an eleven-year-old grandson? Would they be excited, as Brianna had suggested, or would they be disappointed he'd fathered a child out of wedlock? Or maybe both? He guessed the latter. For years his mother had been at him to find a nice girl and settle down and to give her some grandbabies... *but Andy was no baby;* he was almost a teen. But his parents loved God, and they loved people, and so there was no reason why they wouldn't love Andy. They might just be in shock for a while.

Last night, unable to sleep after Brianna went to bed, Andrew had spent the rest of the night in the kitchen preparing not only breakfast, but all the vegetables and everything else for Christmas lunch. He'd told Caitlin earlier what still needed to be done in case he got held up, and while he diced carrots, potatoes and pumpkin, he thought through what it would be like to be a father to Andy. *A real father,* not just a biological father. The prospect scared, yet excited him.

He not only thought, but he prayed, asking God for wisdom. Not only with regard to Andy, but also with Brianna. Andrew hadn't been looking for an instant family, but it seemed highly likely that God had been planning it. Brianna would be the perfect mother for Andy. Kind, caring, understanding, and empathetic. She might not have had any experience with teenagers, but Andrew was sure she'd rise to the challenge. *But was he only interested in her because he'd soon be responsible for a motherless child?* The more he thought and prayed, the more he realised how much he already liked her... dare he say it, *loved her?* But could you love someone you've only just met? All these thoughts and more still ran around his head as he exited the chapel, and he almost bumped into his parents who'd stopped at the door and were putting on coats and scarves.

Andrew pulled himself up, placed Quinn on the stone floor, and helped him into his little coat. Although the chapel was only a short distance from the main house, the day had dawned bitterly cold, and dark, heavy clouds filled the sky. The family had started scampering back to the house to freshen up before Christmas lunch, so as Andrew and his parents followed along behind, he cleared his throat. "Mum, Dad, can we have a chat?"

His parents both slowed. "Sure, son, what's up?" his father asked.

"Let's grab a coffee when we get into the house and find somewhere to talk."

"Is it about you and Brianna?" His mother sounded hopeful.

"Kind of…"

"That sounds promising." Her eyes sparkled.

Andrew gulped. *Yes, but wait until you hear the rest of it.* "I'll make some coffee and we can sit and talk. In the small drawing room?"

"Sure. Sounds intriguing, son." His father angled his head, placing his hand lightly on Andrew's back.

"Yes, well… let me make that coffee. Mum, can you take Quinn? Maybe see if he can play with the other children?"

"My pleasure." His mother flashed a smile and then bent down and took Quinn's hand. "I love the trucks on your sleeves, Quinn."

"Auntie Ash made them." Quinn pointed to his sleeves proudly.

"She's a very clever auntie."

Nodding, Quinn walked off happily with Rosemary.

Andrew headed straight to the kitchen, poured three cups of coffee from the percolator Caitlin had ready, popped them on a tray along with three generous slices of Christmas cake, and walked to the smaller drawing room where his father had already retreated. He stood with his back to the fire. Andrew placed the tray on the coffee table as his mother came into the room. His parents took a seat on the couch while he sat in the single armchair.

"So, son, what is it you need to tell us?" His father leaned back and crossed his legs.

Andrew picked up his coffee and took a slow sip before lifting his gaze, shifting it between his parents. "Do you remember a girl called Shelley that I used to date?"

His mother's brow puckered. "I'm not sure I do." Rosemary turned and looked at her husband, her head tilting in question. "Do you remember her, love?"

Shaking his head, David leaned forward. "Anyway, son, what about her?"

Andrew cleared his throat. "She contacted me recently." Adrenaline surged through his body like a locomotive. Best just to blurt it out and be done with it. "I have an eleven-year old son."

His mother's jaw dropped, her eyes widening. "What do you mean, an eleven-year old son? How do you know he's yours?"

"I thought you'd ask that. I've met him... that's how. He looks exactly like I did at that age. And I've also had a DNA test done."

"So why did this, what did you say her name was?" his father asked, his brows pinching together.

"Shelley... her name's Shelley."

"So why did this Shelley just tell you now? Does she want something from you?" His father sounded disbelieving. Annoyed.

Andrew's shoulders sagged. "Yes, she does." He stared into his coffee mug. "Shelley's dying, and she wants me to take the boy." His heart beat fast as he studied his parents' reactions.

Tears welled in his mother's eyes. "Does the boy know his mother's dying?"

Andrew shook his head. "Not yet, but I'm sure he knows something's wrong."

"How long does she have?" his father asked, taking Rosemary's hand, his voice softening.

"Not long… maybe two months."

"Are you going to take him?" Rosemary dabbed her eyes.

Andrew swallowed hard. "I'm not sure, but I think so."

His father released a heavy sigh. "We never expected this, son, and it will take a while to sink in, but if he *is* your son, then you have to take him. I gather there's no one else lining up for him?"

"No… she hooked up with someone else after we went our own ways, but it didn't last."

"What about her family?" Rosemary asked.

"She hasn't had anything to do with them for years. Her parents are divorced and basically disowned her. Shelley is adamant. She wants me to have him."

His father narrowed his eyes. "How do you feel about that?"

Andrew looked down at his hands. "I was shocked to start with. And angry." Shaking his head, he lifted his gaze, remembering back to the last time he'd seen Shelley. He'd had no idea she was expecting. "If she'd told me she was pregnant, we might have stayed together." Blinking, he wondered whether it would have worked. They were both pretty messed up back then.

"We broke up not long before I went on that walk, but she never said a word."

"It must have been a real surprise." His mother reached out and squeezed his hand.

Andrew nodded. "It took a while, but I finally agreed to meet him. We met in a park, but Shelley didn't tell Andy, that's his name, that I was his dad. She just said I was a friend." Pausing, Andrew glanced out the window before turning and meeting his parents' stunned gazes. "He still doesn't know... she's waiting on my answer before she tells him the truth."

His father's gaze was steady. "And have you decided?"

Andrew's heart pounded so hard he was sure his parents could hear it. Now, it wasn't just something that *might* happen... it was happening. "I've been praying about it a lot, and I feel God wants me to. I'm scared, but excited at the same time."

His father gave him an understanding smile. "I can understand that, especially being on your own."

His mother leaned forward. "How does Brianna fit into the picture. Does she know?"

Andrew blinked. His mother was very perceptive, but was putting him on the spot. "I thought you'd ask that."

"She's a nice girl, Andrew, but can you expect her to be interested in you if you have a son?"

"That's what I thought, but I told her last night, and she's okay with it."

His father's brow furrowed again. "Your having a child by another woman doesn't concern her?"

Andrew shook his head. "No." A slow grin replaced the grim line of his mouth as he recalled the genuine warmth of her reaction. "In fact, she was happy for me."

"Well, sometimes God surprises us with His plans." His

mother chuckled as she dabbed her eyes again. "I was starting to think you were never going to give me any grandchildren, and now we've got an instant one. I'd love to meet him, Andrew. He'll always be welcome here."

Tears stung Andrew's eyes as a deep sense of peace filled his heart. Maybe this really was God's plan for him. "Thanks, Mum. He'd love it here."

David angled his head as a gong sounded. "Is that the dinner bell?"

Andrew glanced at his watch. "I think so. We'd best be going." He stood and raked a trembling hand through his hair. "I'm sorry I shocked you... I was sweating on telling you."

"We all have things in our lives that would surprise others, son." David eased himself up from the couch and then helped Rosemary up. "You needn't have worried." He slipped his arm around her shoulder. "This news has made your mother's day. It's the best Christmas present you could have given her."

Andrew chuckled. "That's what Brianna said you'd say."

"Brianna's a clever girl." His mother moved closer, her eyes shining. "Let me give you a hug." Pulling Andrew close, Rosemary rubbed his back. "You'll make a great father, Andrew."

Coming from his mother, those words were music to his ears. "Thanks, Mum. I appreciate your confidence."

"Come on you two. I don't want to miss my Christmas lunch." David moved to the door, and as he opened it, a flash of red caught Andrew's eye. *Brianna.*

Andrew hurried to the door and poked his head out to call her name. Brianna and Alana both paused and looked back down the hallway. Alana squeezed Brianna's hand and whispered something to her before stepping away and continuing on her way. As his gaze met Brianna's, his heart did a quick flip. Yes, he'd fallen for her big time. He smiled and extended his hand. "Got a second?"

Nodding, Brianna stepped towards him, her gaze shifting between his and his father's.

Andrew slipped an arm around her shoulder and motioned for his father to go back into the room. "Brianna, I've just told Mum and Dad about Andy, and about us..."

"And we're thrilled." His mother stepped forward and gave her a big hug, bringing tears to his eyes. Every minute that passed confirmed this was God's doing.

Letting out a small laugh, Brianna winked at him as she returned his mother's hug. "It's a weekend of surprises."

"It is indeed." Rosemary agreed.

David headed to the door again. "I truly like all this love and togetherness, but we're going to miss our Christmas lunch if we don't go now."

The other three laughed, then they all headed for the dining room.

As Lizzy listened to the happy chatter at the Christmas table, her thoughts drifted. What would life have been like had she married Mathew Carter instead of Daniel? Not for one moment did she regret marrying him, but Mathew had been her first love, and she'd been so looking forward to supporting his ministry as his wife. So much water under the bridge, but there'd been a time when she thought she'd made a mistake marrying Daniel, as had everyone else, given his alcoholism and abuse issues. However, God had brought them through that time, and now she couldn't imagine life without him.

The chat they'd just had following the service made her realise that God had a sense of humour. Daniel had found her when everyone was filing out of the chapel, his eyes alight and full of excitement. "Lizzy, Lizzy love, wait up. I've got something I want to run past you."

She'd stopped and angled her head. "What?"

"I think I know what God wants us to do."

Her eyes widened. They'd been praying for His guidance, but until now, no clear direction had been forthcoming. "Are you going to share?"

"Yes. I think He wants me to be a preacher."

Lizzy laughed. Preaching was a perfect job for Daniel. He loved talking, he was great with people, and he loved God. He was a born communicator, *and God did have a sense of humour.* She, Elizabeth O'Connor, née Walton-Smythe, would be a minister's wife after all. Just not Mathew's wife, but *Daniel's.* Her heart soared, it felt so right. "You'll make a wonderful preacher, Daniel. So... you're thinking Bible College? Four years of study?" Her brow lifted.

"I guess so. I haven't thought that far, but if that's what it takes."

"There's a college near Mother and Father's... maybe we could consider that one?"

Slipping his arms around her waist, Daniel gazed into her eyes. "You'd like that, wouldn't you?"

Lizzy nodded. She loved Scotland and the ruggedness of the Highlands. She loved the people and the ministry they had here, but she missed her home, and her parents would love their grandchildren living near them. "I think it would be perfect."

Daniel leaned forward and kissed her. "Let's pray about it, shall we?"

"Yes. If that's where God wants us, I'm sure He'll show us the way."

"I love you, Liz. Thank you for standing by me when things were bad."

"I love you too, Daniel. God's been good to us."

"He has. Amazingly good."

"So, do we say anything?"

"Not yet... let's keep it our secret for now, but you're on board?"

"Absolutely. You're a born preacher, and God will use you mightily. It feels so right."

When Ryan stood and dinged his glass, Lizzy's thoughts returned to the present. When he announced that he and Grace were expecting a baby and everyone clapped and laughed with elation, Lizzy was so glad she and Daniel had decided not to say anything about their idea just yet. Time enough for that once they were completely sure, although in her mind, there was no doubt.

Over the next few days, while everyone either relaxed indoors or ventured outside when the weather allowed, more news came out. Everyone was initially surprised to hear about Andrew's son, but he and Brianna looked so happy together, it was almost assumed they'd be an instant family before the year was out.

When the time came for everyone to leave, they all agreed it had been the best Christmas ever and they should do it again.

Lizzy didn't say she and Daniel might not be here next Christmas, but the thought raced through her mind that they could have an O'Connor family Christmas at Wivelscombe Manor, her parents' large manor home in the south of England. Wouldn't that be a turn-around!

CHAPTER 16

*B*rianna stood in Lizzy's bedroom in the small cottage at the Elim Community three months later. Lizzy and Grace fussed over her as they adjusted the beautiful lace bridal gown Grace had helped her choose after Andrew proposed less than two weeks after Christmas. She was marrying Andrew McKinnon today, that they were leaving in the morning for their honeymoon in Spain, and that Andy, their eleven-year old son, would be staying here with his new grandparents, Rosemary and David for a holiday in the Highlands. What a whirlwind it had been!

The day Andrew told Andy he was his father was etched in Brianna's memory. Andrew had agreed to meet Shelley and Andy at the restaurant he was the Executive Chef. The day after he returned to Glasgow after the Christmas break, he'd booked the table with the best view of the city—having made the decision and not wanting to waste any time. Shelley would break the news of her terminal condition to her son.

Andrew had asked Brianna to join them, but she believed he needed to do it on his own. He was so nervous that morning, she had to tell him countless times to trust that it would be okay... God was with him and would give him the right words. Brianna promised to stay at her home and pray for them all.

After Andrew left, and all afternoon, Brianna's thoughts and prayers were with them. She tried catching up on some paperwork for the centre to help pass the time, but her heart wasn't in it. Instead, she put on a thick coat and went for a walk, and as she walked, she prayed. Despite the chill of the day, she didn't feel cold. Her focus was totally on Andrew, Shelley and Andy. She pictured how the conversation would go... Andrew's nervousness, and the shock and sorrow in Andy's eyes when he discovered his mother had only months to live. She also imagined his reaction when told that Andrew was his father. Her heart ached for the boy, but she knew that God would wrap him in an invisible blanket of love, protecting his heart. Yes, he'd be sad about his mother, but Andrew was a good man, and would be a great father. He would see Andy through this difficult time.

When Andrew returned to Brianna's semi-attached terraced home several hours later, she'd just put the kettle on and was about to make a pot of tea. As she opened the door, she immediately knew God had answered their prayers. Andrew's eyes sparkled.

She gave him a smile that came from her heart. "So, it went well?"

He nodded enthusiastically, his eyes moistening as he reached out and pulled her close. "Andy said he'd already figured it out."

Brianna couldn't help herself and chuckled. "He sounds like one smart boy."

Andrew pulled back and gazed into her eyes. "He is."

"I'm so glad it went well. What about Shelley? How is she?"

"Are you going to invite me in, or do we have to stand here for all the neighbours to see?"

Brianna chuckled again as she glanced down the street. "Sorry. Come in. I was just making tea. Would you like a cup?"

"Love one."

She'd grabbed his hand and pulled him inside before closing the door. "So, Shelley?"

"He knew about her condition, too. He'd seen her medication and guessed."

"And how is he handling it?" Brianna asked as she poured steaming water into the tea pot.

"Better than expected. But maybe he's putting on a tough front."

"Probably." She took two mugs from the shelf.

"I want you to meet him, Brianna."

She'd turned around and faced him. "Isn't it too soon?"

Andrew had stepped toward her, rubbing her forearms with his, and gazed deeply into her eyes. "I know we haven't known each other long, but I love you, Brianna. I love everything about you, and I want to spend my life with you. I just know it deep down that this is right. Brianna, will you marry me?"

Her palm had flown to her chest, where she felt her heart lurch. Never in a million years had she expected their relationship to accelerate so quickly. But she'd agreed... it seemed so right. Joy bubbled in her laugh as she'd nodded eagerly. "Yes,

Andrew McKinnon, I'll marry you!" she'd exclaimed. She'd gazed into his eyes, and as his arms encircled her, she'd buried her hands in his hair, lifted her face, and waited for his passionate kiss. Her knees weakened as his lips, warm and sweet, met hers.

Two days later, Brianna met Andy and she loved him immediately. He was just like his father, not only in looks, but in personality, soft and gently spoken, courteous and polite. But she knew deep down there would be sadness and loss, and plenty of challenges to overcome. She prayed that God would help her and Andrew to be sensitive, and to help Andy through the difficult days ahead.

They agreed not to wait to marry. They were both sure, and so now, here she was, preparing to marry her perfect man.

"There," Grace said as she stood after adjusting Brianna's long train. "You look beautiful, Bibi." Holding her at arm's length, Grace gazed into her eyes. "I'm so happy for you."

Brianna forced herself not to cry—she didn't want to ruin her make-up. Instead, she swallowed hard and returned Grace's smile. "Thank you, Grace. For everything. I mean it."

"Come on now, enough of that, or we'll both be blubbering messes. Time to get you hitched."

Brianna laughed gently. Yes, it was time to get hitched.

LIZZY SAT in the Elim Community chapel, her heart over-flowing with love and gratitude as Daniel walked down the aisle with Brianna's arm tucked through his. She was a beautiful bride, her face was glowing, and it warmed Lizzy's heart to see how much in love she and Andrew were.

Brianna's eyes were firmly fixed on Andrew, looking ruggedly handsome in McKinnon clan tartan, but when Lizzy caught Daniel's eye as he and Brianna passed and he winked at her, she couldn't help but smile. New beginnings were everywhere. Brianna was marrying Andrew, eleven-year old Andy had a new family, Grace and Ryan were expecting their first child, and she and Daniel were looking forward to moving closer to her parents and him starting Bible College in a few weeks' time.

And then there was Alana. Caitlin had taken Daniel's younger sister under her wing when they both returned to Belfast after Christmas, and Alana seemed at peace. Happy, even. God was working in her life as He no doubt was in the lives of the others. They might not have responded to Him yet, but Daniel and Lizzy prayed for Shawn, Brendan, Aislin and Joel every night, along with all his other siblings. They'd become so close since Christmas, and even Brendan had flown back to Scotland for Brianna's wedding, having managed to stay out of jail for the longest time ever.

So many things to be thankful for. So many blessings. So much to look forward to. Lizzy sighed with contentment as Daniel joined her and squeezed her hand. They were indeed blessed beyond measure.

"Every good and perfect gift is from above, coming down from the Father of the heavenly lights, who does not change like shifting shadows." James 1:17

NOTE FROM THE AUTHOR

I hope you enjoyed Brianna and Andrew's heartwarming story as much as I enjoyed writing it. If you have yet to read the first four books of "The Shadows Series", read them now to discover how Danny's, Lizzy's, Grace's and Brianna's stories began! The first three books are Daniel and Lizzy's story and are available in a Box Set which is also free to read on Kindle Unlimited. Book 4, "Secrets and Sacrifice", is Grace's story and is available separately, and can also be read as a stand-alone.

Make sure you don't miss my new releases by joining my mailing list. **Visit www.julietteduncan.com/subscribe** to join, and as a thank you for signing up, you'll also receive a **free short story.**

Finally, could I ask you a favor? Would you help other people find this book by writing a review and telling them why you liked it? Honest reviews of my books help bring them to the attention of other readers just like yourself, and I'd be very grateful if you could spare just five minutes to leave a review (it can be as short as you like).

With gratitude,

Juliette

ALSO BY JULIETTE DUNCAN

The Shadows Series www.julietteduncan.com/the-shadows-series/

Book 1: Lingering Shadows

To her family's consternation, Lizzy deals with heartache by running away with Daniel, a near-stranger. Once they're married, Lizzy discovers her new husband has demons he hasn't shared with her-- and the stresses of marriage will send him back to them.

Book 2: Facing the Shadows

Daniel is locked in a downward spiral, unable to break free of his demons. Though her heart aches for him, Lizzy realizes she must protect herself and their unborn child. She must also face her own past before she turns toward the future. When Daniel is badly injured by his own folly, can this couple who've been divided by pain, embrace God's healing touch on them both?

Book 3: Beyond the Shadows

Lizzy and Daniel settle into their new life in the Lake District. As Daniel grows in his faith, they look forward to parenthood. But when Daniel receives devastating news of a family tragedy, his sobriety is threatened. As he and Lizzy travel to Ireland to reunite with his estranged family, can Daniel draw on God's strength and Lizzy's support to remain a steadfast man of faith?

Book 4: Secrets and Sacrifice

When Grace O'Connor arrives in the Scottish Highlands, she's hiding a secret and trailing more baggage than she cares to admit. Grace's sister, Brianna, has a history linked to Grace's secret. There, amongst the rugged Scottish Highlands and a community of caring, loving Christians, Grace meets the handsome Ryan MacGregor, an ex-military Paratrooper with a history of his own. As the secrets of Grace's past unravel and the sacrifices she's made are thrown back at her, Grace faces the biggest decision of her life. As everything she has believed is turned upside down, Grace realizes that the walls she's worked so hard at building have been for no reason whatsoever, and she now needs to discover who the real Grace O'Connor is.

The True Love Series

After her long-term relationship falls apart, Tessa Scott is left questioning God's plan for her life, and she's feeling vulnerable and unsure of how to move forward.

Ben Williams is struggling to keep the pieces of his life together after his wife of fourteen years walks out on him and their teenage son. Tessa's housemate inadvertently sets up a meeting between the two of them, triggering a chain of events neither expected. Be prepared for a roller-coaster ride of emotions as Tessa, Ben and Jayden do life together and learn to trust God to meet their every need.

The Precious Love Series Book 1 - Forever Cherished

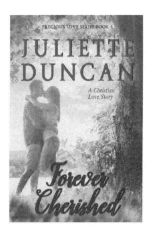

"Forever Cherished" is a stand-alone novel, but follows on from "The True Love Series" books. Now Tessa is living in the country, she wants to share her and Ben's blessings with others, but when a sad, lonely woman comes to stay, Tessa starts to think she's bitten off more than she can chew, and has to rely on her faith at every turn. Leah Maloney is carrying a truck-load of disappointments and has almost given up on life. Her older sister arranges for her to spend time at 'Misty Morn', but Leah is suspicious of her sister's motives.

Praise for "Forever Cherished"

"Another amazing story of God's love and the amazing ways he works in our lives." Ruth H

Hank and Sarah - A Love Story, *the Prequel to "The Madeleine Richards Series" is a FREE thank you gift for joining my mailing list. You'll also be the first to hear about my next books and get exclusive sneak previews. Get your free copy at www.julietteduncan.com/subscribe*

The Madeleine Richards Series Although the 3 book series is intended mainly for pre-teen/Middle Grade girls, it's been read and enjoyed by people of all ages.

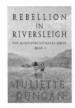 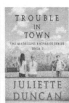

ABOUT THE AUTHOR

Juliette Duncan is a Christian fiction author, passionate about writing stories that will touch her readers' hearts and make a difference in their lives. Although a trained school teacher, Juliette spent many years working alongside her husband in their own business, but is now relishing the opportunity to follow her passion for writing stories she herself would love to read. Based in Brisbane, Australia, Juliette and her husband have five adult children, seven grandchildren, and an elderly long haired dachshund.Apart from writing, Juliette loves exploring the great world we live in, and has travelled extensively, both within Australia and overseas. She also enjoys social dancing and eating out.

Connect with Juliette:

Email: juliette@julietteduncan.com

Website: www.julietteduncan.com

Facebook: www.facebook.com/JulietteDuncanAuthor

Twitter: https://twitter.com/Juliette_Duncan

Made in the USA
Middletown, DE
14 June 2021